TWICE BURNED

RONALD GETTEL

TWICE BURNED

WALKER AND COMPANY
NEW YORK

To Ruth Cavin

The author gratefully acknowledges the
help of David Sobel (associate editor)
and Patti Gettel (inspiration-in-residence)

First published in the United States of America in
1983 by the Walker Publishing Company, Inc.

Published simultaneously in Canada by John Wiley
& Sons Canada, Limited, Rexdale, Ontario.
ISBN: 0-8027-5485-6
ISBN: 0-8027-5498-8 Special Edition

Design by Laura Ferguson
Library of Congress Catalog Card Number:
82-61792
Printed in the United States of America

10 9 8 7 6 5 4 3 2 1

Folks, look. *This is fiction. Okay, so some of the background and locations in the story are real. And, believe me, I'm painfully aware that some of the events in the story have since come true. I put it to you: Is that* my *fault? Folks, I'll say the word one more time:* fiction. *And if any more of this story comes true, well, I don't want to hear about it.*

1

NIGHT LIGHTS

CHICAGO's north side is shaped a lot like a fat lady's leg, as seen from the side. On the front of her leg, on the east, Lake Michigan kisses her thigh along Loyola Park, pats her knee at Lincoln Park, caresses her shin up and down Lake Shore Drive, and wets her toes at Navy Pier. The Chicago River runs down the back of her leg and right out under her foot. The City of Chicago started at her instep and was groping its way quickly up her leg when America's most famous hotfoot caught her by the heel and burned just about everything off her foot, her ankle, and part of her calf. Ah, but the old appeal is still there; various ethnic groups take turns playing with her leg. She wears precious jewels—the Drake, Marina City, Hancock Tower, Water Tower Place—to adorn her foot, and she wears the Gold Coast up the front of her ankle. But there are also ugly bruises on her leg, and a vast Malthusian growth hard up behind her threatens to turn her streets into running wounds.

Pulling away from Robert Hammond's apartment building on the Gold Coast and heading west, they drove over former lakebed, over land that was almost perfectly flat. However, in economic and social terms, they rolled down a mountainside. Away from lakefront living that is in some ways the most elegant in the

Midwest; then between rows of old town houses; next along detached dwellings built only a few feet apart; on past some of the meanest public housing to be found anywhere; and into a belt of old plants and warehouses along the North Branch of the Chicago River.

The drive took seven minutes. With the Mars lights going, clearing the few night drivers out of the way, it would have taken less time, but Gault's driver was braking almost to a stop at every intersection. Was he lost? What the hell's the *matter* with this driver? Hammond was tempted to ask. But didn't. "Ah, excessive politeness," he chided himself, "The Curse of the Hammonds."

When they were six blocks away, Hammond could see it. Three blocks away, he could smell it. Two blocks, hear it. They parked, walked at it.

It was a furnace. A raging, block-long, three-story-high light show. Red and yellow making orange. White streams of water giving off colored mist. Wet pavement bleeding the colors of the fire. Blinking lights sweeping across the dark buildings away from the fire.

And noise. Roaring and growling, the fire ate with its mouth open. Timbers cracking, falling. Popping. Flapping. Windows blowing out. The high-pitched complaining of superheated air being forced through small openings. The rude noises made by radios switching on and off to give their messages. A siren, coming closer. Voices and coughing: the punier sounds of men.

And heat. Heat that made it hard to breathe, yet made you want to smoke. Hammond wanted to smoke but decided not to. Not yet.

The driver led him to a white command bus parked on the cross street at the far end of the block and held the door open for him to enter. Hammond stepped up into the brightly lighted interior. He was momentarily grateful for the cool air. Damn July. The only man inside who was not wearing a uniform gave Hammond a nod of recognition and began to move forward to greet him.

A tuxedo. Who but Gault would show up at an extra-alarm fire in the middle of the night in a tuxedo? Yet on Minot Winston Gault III, a tuxedo somehow became the proper uniform. He had almost-too-white hair and an aristocratic air that would fit in in an ad for a Corniche or a bottle of Taittinger's. A fat officer not quite in Gault's path took an exaggerated step back—deference to the commissioner—and Hammond remembered films of Hermann Göring clucking around his *Führer.*

Gault showed his well-tended teeth and dropped a manicured hand lightly on Hammond's shoulder. "Hammond. Good, *good.*"

"Sir."

Gault's well-modulated voice said, "Let's take a walk, Rob," and Göring got the door.

Stepping back down onto the night street, Hammond noticed that some of the hose streams were being turned away from the fire and onto the dark buildings nearby. Concede the block that's burning if you have to, but no more. He and Gault turned their backs on the fire and began to walk, with no destination, down a side street. They stepped around rivulets of water coming away from the fire, and the pavement pulled at their shoes like chewing gum.

Thousands of spiders crawled on the lake side of the building. Tens of thousands. The size of half dollars, only *fat.* And somehow, amazingly, these fat devils were able to squeeze inside, in through cracks around the glass doors that could be opened to Hammond's balcony. And as if the spider invasion were not nightmarish enough, it was being followed by a *second* invasion: Swarms of wasps, the spiders' natural enemies, were out there building nests on the balconies.

Ten minutes after Hammond had gotten the call from Gault's driver and hurried out of his sixth-floor condominium flat, Sheri Sue had finished dressing and was leaving it. Her turquoise eyes were opened wide as she walked jerkily across the living room, on the lookout for spiders. At the door she spun swiftly. Had she heard something? Nothing she could see. Surely you couldn't hear a spider, not on *carpet,* anyway. She quick-stepped into the corridor and yanked the door shut behind her, then let out a long breath and sagged back against the door, holding the knob for support.

Terrified though she was of the spiders, Sheri Sue was not leaving Hammond's flat because she chose to. Hammond had insisted; when she had protested, he had invoked "our agreement." ("Remember *our agreement,* Sheri Sue. We don't live together, and at the office we hardly know each other.") As she leaned there against the door, tears came and she thought defiantly: *Your* agreement. *Your* agreement, Robert V. Hammond, not mine.

She became aware of the slap, slap, slapping that meant old Trash Truck was coming. Aw, *no.* Sheri Sue was about to be disapproved of again. Trash Truck was a moustachioed woman who lived somewhere down the corridor. Hammond had given her the nickname, not alone because of her appearance—although once you stopped to think about it, she *was* shaped remarkably like the refuse trucks that grumbled around Chicago— but because the woman seemed always to be on her way to, or just returning from, the trash-chute room. She seldom failed to make a trash run whenever Sheri Sue appeared outside Hammond's door, for the sole purpose, Sheri Sue believed, of disapproving of Sheri Sue. Hammond was skeptical about this last part, but then he'd never seen those twin death rays of disapproval. She must keep a hundred bags of trash inside her front door, just waiting for the call. Hammond and Sheri Sue often speculated about what was in all of those bags she put down the chute. Spiders and wasps? Or love letters from masochists? Maybe paralyzed men who got a look at her without that dowdy housecoat on. On two occasions, Sheri Sue had tried speaking to Trash Truck but had gotten no response—absolutely *none*—except for the death rays. Slap, slap, slap. Sheri Sue wiped the back of a hand across her eyes and looked toward the sound, saw what she knew she would see. A bag carrying a bag. Slippers attacking feet. And disapproval. As Trash Truck slapped up with the death rays blazing, Sheri Sue adjusted the positioning of her bra with a theatrical flourish. *"Men!"* she said to a stunned Trash Truck and swiveled down the corridor toward the elevators. A man stepping out of an elevator turned completely around as he walked past Sheri Sue, reluctant to take his eyes from such beauty, and collided with Trash Truck.

In the dimly lit street, Gault's tuxedo shirt seemed to glow faintly. Gault described the collision, letting one hand represent the ladder truck and the other hand the squad car. The ladder truck had struck the squad car broadside, driving it across the intersection and squashing it against a private auto.

Hammond stopped walking and lit a cigarette. So

that's why Gault's driver had brought him here at half speed.

"How bad was it, sir?"

"Fireman will probably live. The policeman's dead. The woman, she just had some minor injuries."

"Where did they, uh, come together?"

"Clybourn and something—North, I think. It's being investigated right now—by *cops*."

"Both units called, both on their way to *this* fire?" Hammond said.

"Yes."

"To say the obvious, the question about whether one of the drivers was at fault, that doesn't help. No rain, no fog—"

"No, it doesn't help."

Gault began to walk again, and Hammond followed his lead.

"When they circumcised *that* boy, they threw away the wrong piece."

That's what the presentence investigator had told the juvenile judge. (With less candor, she cited "sociopathic attitudes" in her written report.) Her recommendation was that the boy be placed in an institutional setting—a *secure* setting. Despite which advice, the judge gave the boy a suspended sentence.

But that happened ten years ago and two states away. And besides, no one could know about that here in Chicago because the boy's juvenile records had been sealed.

For the boy's protection.

Safely home now, he felt the tightness begin to thaw. He drew off his gloves with exaggerated care. Then he held up his hands and examined them, worked the fingers. Still hard to believe sometimes. A look at these mitts would make an undertaker flinch. In one of his early Chicago arsons, the accelerant was accidently ignited while he was still spreading it, and he was hideously burned. The flesh on his hands had cooked like a pudding; viscous bubbles rose and broke with a *blup!* and, without benefit of stirring, cooled into amorphous lumps. Later the fingers had had to be surgically cut apart. Now his hands rather resembled pincers, if they looked much like anything. Even so, one could argue that he had been lucky. He had not died in that fire (an eighty-one-year-old black woman and her two-year-old great-granddaughter, both of whom looked much too small to be decently put into full-sized body bags, *had*); he had gotten away; he had not been connected with the fire. Yes, lucky.

Suddenly he'd had enough of thinking about his hands, thought instead about how it had been tonight. Parking four blocks away and walking to a Wabash drugstore and buying ten packages of condoms. Sneaking into the Clybourn Street building. Filling each condom so carefully. Deciding where to hang each one. The odor of gasoline. The edge of fear that revved his heart and made his penis retract into his body as far as it could go. He visualized each condom bursting and spilling out its burden onto the small "starter" fires. He thought about the policemen and firemen who must be going crazy right now trying to cope with what *he* had done. Of people in the crowd wondering who in the hell did *this*.

Whenever he thought about those sicko's who built pathetic little fires and then stood around them with glassy eyes and hard-ons, he was revulsed. Really sickened. They gave the professionals a foul image, and he

• 7 •

was a professional. One hundred and three arsons as of tonight, only for money—as much per pop now as you paid a professional killer. And why not? You go look up "professional," as he had, and you'd see he was just as professional as any one of those guys who played sports for Chicago. If he screwed up as often as *they* did . . .

Before he went out again into the small hours of Tuesday morning, he scrubbed himself and dressed in clean clothes, other shoes. He knew that arson investigators had oil-soluble dyes they could put on your clothes or on your shoes, even on your *skin,* to see if there were traces of oil or gasoline there. He knew about such things. He drew on clean gloves; he always wore gloves when he went out where he might be seen.

2

MO-BILIZING

"CALL me 'Mo.' "

"Moe, sir?"

"You know, em-oh. Short for Minot."

"Oh, *sure.*" Mo was one of the Three Stooges, wasn't he? A ludicrous nickname for this elegant-looking man pacing along beside him in a tuxedo. Hammond was beginning to feel wary. Was he being courted by this important man? Get to the point, Gault, get to the point.

"Rob, I want you to help me, help me pick the right man to handle this fire investigation."

"Sure. Of course, Mo."

"Fasulo was in here early. He thinks maybe more than one fire, separate fires. So maybe arson, maybe an arsonist who caused the death of a policeman. Now, if anybody is ever going to make a case out of this, how vital will it be to prove the arson part?"

"Essential, as you know. If you can't prove the corpus of arson, you've *got* no case. None at all, no matter what else you *can* prove."

"So we need the best man we can get."

"The best." Hammond's mind was sorting candidates.

"And who *is* the best, Rob?"

"Probably Osdick—"

"No good."

"—or Potts."

"Even worse."

"Now, hold on here. I don't—"

"Rob, how many cases of arson did we have last year?"

Hammond was stung by Gault's disdain for his recommendations—and for two firemen he respected—and he was put off balance momentarily by the abrupt change in tack. He tried to read Gault's face in the dark. Wherever Gault was going with this, it was as if he had already worked it all out, as if this performance were solely for Hammond's benefit.

"You know the answer to that as well as I do."

"Tell me."

"Well, as you *know*, Commissioner—"

"Mo."

"Mo!" Hammond's anger flashed. Here he was, in the middle of the night, saying his ABC's for this man who spit on his suggestions, a guy in a tux who wanted to be called Mo, while they walked *away* from an extra-alarm fire. Jesus! He waited a bit before continuing, letting the silence tell of his anger.

"As you *know*, Mo, nobody knows how many arsons we have, not really. Fires destroy a lot of evidence. So do the firemen who put them out. And eyewitnesses are rare. If you really want to know how many arsons, it's simple; just put a well-trained investigator on every fire. Only just the one small problem, forgive me for bringing it up: You have a hundred, two hundred fires a day, and you only have enough people to study just a few of them."

"So we have the people—the same men you train, Rob—to put into a fire, fight it, carry the victims out, maybe get carried out themselves, but we don't have the people to tell us if that fire was set on purpose?"

Hammond made no response.

"That about it, Rob?"

"More or less."

"Rob, do you *know* the guys who're handling arson now?"

"Well, it's been changed around some since I had anything to do with that end of it, but, essentially, it's up to the police now, the Bomb and Arson Squad. Some firemen are assigned to them to help determine cause-of-fire. If the cops can make an arrest, then it's up to the state's attorney."

"And how's it working?"

"They've had some successes."

Gault jerked around to face Hammond. There was enough light in the night street to show a vein standing out on Gault's forehead, and the force of his gaze surprised Hammond. Then Gault erupted.

"Horseshit! *You* know the arsonists come and go as they please in Chicago. *I* know it." Gault's words boiled out, his hands were going. "And what the hell do we catch and convict? A little kid walking down the street with a gas can in one hand and a siphon in the other. An ex-boyfriend who's out of his tree. Some pathetic loser who's gassed to the guardrails. *That's* who we catch. But a pro, or an amateur who's under control? Shit! And every time a fireman gets killed, or even gets hurt, I get more fucking fed up with it! And I need some *help*, goddamnit."

Gault had thrown his script away; the man was plainly in a rage. Hammond was touched by this unexpected show of anger and pain.

"How can I help, Mo?"

"Handle the investigation of this fire."

Involuntarily, Hammond drew back. "*That's* the point of all this?" Hammond was irritated with Gault for being devious and was disgusted with himself for being so goddamned dense. "Commissioner, I'm the *drillmaster*. And when I took over at the Fire Academy, it was specifically agreed—"

Gault put a hand on Hammond's forearm. "Chief, you don't know what's involved."

Hammond caught the shift to "Chief," wondered if he was being reminded that he was subordinate to Gault. Or was it a reminder that "Drillmaster" was not his only title?

Gault's voice was under control, modulated again. "There's more at stake here than you know, Rob. The insurance companies have been on the mayor's ass, really hard. And the state's attorney's. They see the success of some other anti-arson efforts, like those task forces in Houston, Seattle. Well, when it comes to politics, my boy, the insurance companies are high-rafter bats. They got the mayor's attention, and they got the state's attorney's attention. So we've been meeting for six, seven weeks trying to work out a trial program for a sort of super task force against arson. And we've been wrestling with the same old crap: Who is responsible for what, and who's in charge? Cops don't know doodledy-squat about fires, firemen don't know how to catch crooks, and there are legal problems. And trying to get the cops and firemen to really cooperate is about like getting two bulls to mate. But guess what? If there has to be a new task force, every-goddamn-body wants to be in *charge* of it."

Hammond said quietly, "I can think of one exception."

Gault did not acknowledge Hammond's comment. Gault waited a moment, then resumed. He told Hammond it had been agreed that a state's attorney, a fellow named Kleinschmidt, should be in administrative charge, but the question of who would be the *active* head, the guy who would run the day-to-day investigations, wasn't settled. This new outfit—they hadn't even agreed on a name—would concentrate on certain fires, certain people. Gault had tentatively offered Osdick and a couple of backup men, but would have no problem substituting a man for Osdick. Kleinschmidt specifically asked for a cop named Benedetto, a lieutenant, and the cops jumped at that and agreed to furnish some other men.

"This man Benedetto is very young, only thirty-something—don't screw up your face, Rob; that's very young to *me*—and doesn't know the first thing about fires, maybe *saw* one once. But Kleinschmidt thinks the guy can do anything, so the cops assume Benedetto'll be the man in charge. And he *will* be if Osdick is the alternative."

"You say this Benedetto's a lieutenant? Osdick has a higher rank."

"I'm afraid that's not enough. I've met Benedetto, and he is tough. He's had a lot of successes with vice, homicide, and it's partly because people are afraid of him—I mean literally *afraid* of him. Even some of the other *cops* won't have anything to do with *this* cop. Well, Kleinschmidt *loves* the guy, *asked* for him. In an organization like this, there aren't clear-cut rules and precedents; rank's a help, but it's no guarantee. And to this Benedetto, a guy like Osdick would be a light snack."

"Well, I assume that you have some time to consider others."

"We're talking about *tonight,* Rob. We were getting to the final stages of organization and then *this* thing happened." Gault held his right hand up, a foot in front of his face, and with his thumb and forefinger extended three inches apart, traced an imaginary headline on the front page of the *Tribune* and "read" aloud, "FIREMAN KILLS COP ON WAY TO FIRE."

Gault had talked with the mayor, and he was hot, hot

as Gault had seen him in all the years he'd been close to the man. The mayor talked with Kleinschmidt, and the decision was made: Start now. No more meetings, no more discussions.

"We just *do* it. There's no question about that, Rob. There *is* a question about who runs what."

"Is that really so all-important, Mo? For *us* to run this thing?"

Without hesitation, Gault said, "Yes."

"Well, with due respect, I'm not sure I see that. The best men I've ever met in my life are firemen, but I don't think they're the *only* ones with brains—"

"Agreed."

"—or courage—"

"Agreed."

"—and as you just pointed out yourself, Mo, we're short of people to do the work we've got *now*. What's wrong with letting somebody *help* us?"

"We can use a lot of help, Rob. Nevertheless, there are several damned good reasons why we ought to be in charge of this thing. In the first place, protecting the people of Chicago from fire has always been the job of the Fire Department. You want the cops running *that*?"

"Chasing lawbreakers has always been *their* job, Mo. Somebody has to give up just a little authority here." Hammond was reasoning more than arguing.

"Secondly, our image, the Fire Department's image, has been gradually going right down the tubes. Remember how it was when you first came in, Rob? Everybody trusted a fireman—hell, *loved* the guy. Then there was that fuss about how we didn't have enough blacks. Then it was fire inspectors taking bribes, and then the strike really did it up. The point is, Rob, that this new effort may get a lot of publicity, *good* publicity, and having a fireman at the head of it could help *all* firemen.

"Thirdly, I think this might help us when we go in on our next budget. I don't need to tell you; you write manuals used all over the country, and we can't even afford to buy enough copies for your own students right here in Chicago.

"And, Rob, it isn't *cops* that get carried out of arson fires. Nobody knows what arson costs Chicago like a fireman who sees firemen carried out.

"The mayor and Kleinschmidt know who you are and can't take you lightly. If you make a statement to the press, it's coming from a chief who's a hero and an authority. Rob, this needs you. You've got the brains. You've got the bugles. I think you've got the balls. Have you?"

"Ah, a challenge to my manliness, huh? *That's* what you choose for the main thrust? With no disrespect, sir, I believe the part I liked the best was, how did it go, 'carrying out firemen'?"

A smile of frank approval spread over Gault's face. "You give this all you've got, Rob, and I'll back you. And Rob—"

"Yes?"

"I've got balls, too."

Hammond threw up a hand as if to forestall some dreaded action by Gault. "I'll take your word for it, sir."

Gault laughed and clapped Hammond on the back. The two men turned and began walking again, back toward the fire. A whimsical thought danced into Hammond's mind; on some other dark street at this very moment, was the police commissioner giving Lieutenant Benedetto a last-minute pep talk, too?

3

OPENING ROUNDS

IF Auguste Rodin had taken a five-foot-high block of granite and chiseled out the form of a man by cutting away as little stone as possible, he might have sculpted a fair likeness of Dominic Benedetto. Benedetto had no neck, no waist, only the suggestions of ankles. Hammond was awed by the man's aura of strength—Jesus Christ, even the guy's *hair* looked strong—but Hammond tried not to let it show; this was a time to play poker.

Benedetto had a voice that rumbled up from somewhere deeper than his throat: "I feel real lucky havin' you *assist* me on this—"

Hammond made a surgical cut through Benedetto's sentence: "We'll have time for amenities later. This is a critical time in an arson investigation. Can you come with me now?"

"Uh, yeah."

Benedetto had been maneuvered and he knew it, but he also knew that Hammond was the expert at the fire scene and had the advantage here. Benedetto had lost the first round, but his time would come, soon, if he could get Hammond alone.

Benedetto looked at Kleinschmidt, a skinny man whose eyes told the world he was nobody to fool with.

Kleinschmidt nodded to Benedetto, dismissal and good-bye. Kleinschmidt and Gault exchanged a look but said nothing.

Hammond stepped down out of the brightly lit command bus and began walking toward the fire, haltingly because his eyes were adjusting to the dim light. Benedetto trailed close behind the drillmaster for several yards. With no warning, Benedetto stopped, caught Hammond's upper arm in a cruel grip, and yanked the tall man full around to face him. Hammond was disoriented—startled to be suddenly flying, to be feeling ripping pain, to be facing the massive Benedetto. Benedetto held the painful grip and rumbled, "You ever try shuttin' off my water like that again, I'll bury my foot about three feet up yer ass." Then, abruptly, Benedetto released Hammond's arm, smiled as if they were comrades, and said, "Now that we have *that* shit out of the way, what do I call you? Bob?"

Hammond knew he was no physical match for this short monster, and he didn't have anything to knock him down with. His most urgent wish was to be somewhere else suddenly so he could hold his arm and not keep denying the pain. With his teeth set, Hammond managed to say, "Call me Chief."

Benedetto parodied great awe by tilting his head back, opening his eyes wide, holding his hands out as if presenting Hammond to a group of spectators, and drawing the word out in a reverential tone. "C . . . h . . . i . . . e . . . e . . . f . . . f ! Oh, wow, thank you, Chieeeff!"

Hammond tried to steer the confrontation in a different direction. "How many men do you have here now, Lieutenant?"

Benedetto's voice sounded too deep for a human's voice. "Two." He was grinning, In the night street, Benedetto had the whip hand.

"Any more assigned to the—uh—task force?"

"Not yet, but I can get 'em if I feel we need 'em."

"Okay, Benedetto, here's the way this works. While waiting for you to get here, I made up a list of things I'll need. I want you to get them, all of them, exactly as I've listed them, and get them here *fast*. Before you go, I want you to have your two—the two men report to me, and I'll tell them what I want them to do while you're gone."

Hammond handed his list to Benedetto.

Again the grin. "Well, I'll send one of my men for yer stuff and—"

"No! I want *you* to go, Benedetto, and I want you to go *now*."

Benedetto stopped grinning. He came a step closer, again violating the distance by which civil men normally stand apart, and looked up into Hammond's eyes. Very slowly, he raised the massive hand which held Hammond's list until it was inches from Hammond's eyes. He took his time crumpling the paper into a wad and then opened his hand and let the wad fall. During this, he did not move his eyes from Hammond's eyes.

"Sure I will, Chieeeff. Right after I see you go sit in that fire."

Hammond turned and held his hand out toward the fire. The fire appeared to have lost some of its youthful energy, but it still had fight left in it. "You really think you ought to be in charge of *this*?"

"I don't know much about fire investigations—yet," said Benedetto, "so I'm willin' to work *with* you. I'm no messenger boy, and as far as I know, nobody put you in charge of anythin'. I know you're not in charge of me. Or my men."

Big generous deal, thought Hammond; now this Neanderthal is willing to work *with* me. "Well, you're right about one thing, Benedetto; you don't know much about fire investigations. There are, let's see, five things you need to know about *this* fire investigation." Hammond held up his hands, used his right hand to keep count on the fingers of his left hand.

The right hand gripped the left thumb. "*One.* Count the bugles, Lieutenant."

Then the index finger. "*Two.* Technically, the Fire Department is going to remain in charge of this fire scene until I study it. Then it's going to give it back to whomever owns it or occupies—occupied—it. If I give orders to bar you, and I will, you can't get within a block of the scene."

Then the middle finger. "*Three. I'm* going to study the fire scene. Nobody else. If I do that alone, any case will depend on my report and on the possibility of my testimony."

Then the ring finger. "*Four.* Right now, what we need worst is the stuff on that list. That's why I told *you* to go."

And the little finger. "*Five.* If you leave right now, Benedetto, you might be able to get that stuff together for me and get back here before it's time to go in. If you don't leave right now, I'll send a fireman and you're *out*, at least out of this phase of it. You and your men. Do you want to stand around playing with yourself for a day or two, or do you want to do what I tell you? Decide right now."

Benedetto did not change expression. He bent over and retrieved the crumpled paper. The move was surprisingly agile for a man of his mass. The paper had water and mud on it, but Benedetto opened it, laid it on the front of his suit coat, and smoothed it with hands that looked strong enough to break stones, giving Hammond obeisance.

"I'd like to stand here and talk with you, Chieeeff, but I really gotta go get some stuff."

Benedetto had lost round two. However, Dominic

Benedetto was a fighter who could absorb punishment in the early rounds if he had to and still knock your head off at the end.

The fire was darkening, terminal. One hour, maybe two before Hammond could go inside the building. Enough time. We'll be ready, thought Hammond. But he was tired and he was having trouble not thinking about the unwelcome changes in his life.

It took ten minutes to set up "the office." When the two police officers reported to him shortly after Benedetto's departure, Hammond led them to a location he had chosen a block north of the fire, a spot with a view of the fire scene. Then he sent one of the policemen to drive a car there to serve as his temporary office. He dispatched the other policeman to report this location to the command bus and then to locate the nearest telephone and the nearest rest room.

Hammond used the next twenty minutes to talk with the two men—each individually, privately in "the office"—and to give them their assignments. To Detective Sergeant Vernon Hooker, who had more years and more confidence, Hammond gave the responsibility of writing down the license number of every vehicle in the neighborhood and the name of every person within two blocks. He told Hooker to make notes on anyone's unusual appearance or behavior. Was some man dressed oddly, too carefully perhaps, for 2:00 A.M. in this neighborhood? Was some woman emotionally worked up? Even if a person said he knew nothing at all about the fire, *nothing,* Hooker was to get it down in writing. Hammond knew that a person who told you he knew nothing at all might show up at a trial a year later as a witness for the defendant. Hammond also knew the odds against finding a credible eyewitness at the fire scene, but he didn't tell Hooker.

The other man, Detective Sergeant Dennis Rosewater, was small for a cop and had a smooth, almost feminine complexion. Hammond told him to call in a request for a photographer and to make certain the man was there and ready to go to work in an hour. Next, he was to find out who owned the burning property—the big computer in Daley Center should have it or, if not, a car could be sent out for somebody who works in the assessor's office—and to try to get the owner down there. Rosewater would then assist Hooker and later on would bring coffee and food for the squad and for the firemen who would be posted to guard the fire scene against intruders.

Hammond told each man that a policeman had been killed as a direct result of this fire, and he could see it in their faces: They hadn't known before. He asked for their most dedicated help tonight, and it was clear from their responses that he would get it. He told them that working at a fire scene—with policemen and firemen and even politicians giving orders and with reporters asking questions—might become confusing for them; that they were now acting under his, Hammond's, authority, and that they should bring any problems to him, *directly* to him. To make it clear who was in charge, Hammond told each man that he had sent Benedetto on an errand and that, as soon as that man saw Benedetto, he was to tell Benedetto to report to him here at "the office."

Next, Hammond went to find Fasulo. It wasn't hard. When Fasulo was in charge of men fighting a fire, it was obvious to anybody with eyes and ears. Hammond stopped a few paces away from Fasulo, who was in conversation with two junior officers, their heads close together because of the noise. Hammond did not want to interrupt them, to interfere in any way with their work; first you get the people out (if you can), next you make sure the fire isn't going to get out of control (if you can), then you put the fire out (if you can), and *then* you investigate (if you can). Hammond regarded Fasulo affectionately as Fasulo tried to stand still to talk to his men, fighting against what—hyperkinesis? Hammond didn't spend much time with the combat officers now, but before he had moved over to the Academy and begun the extra teaching and the writing, he had passed many good evenings talking, drinking, laughing with this fidgety clown.

Hammond saw that one of the younger officers had appeared to recognize him, inclining his head in Hammond's direction and saying something to Fasulo. Fasulo's big head turned, and his smoke-and-soot-blackened face broke open into a grin. He arched his back and slapped both hands on his helmet. The fire was under control, and it was now showtime.

"Oh, no! Stand up straight, men, for chrissakes, the *teacher's* here! Get them hoses up off the street before you get 'em dirty! *Right* hand, Johnson, *right* hand; you hold the hose with your right hand, an' you abuse yourself with your left hand!"

Without warning, Fasulo, whose turnout coat was caked with crud and streaming water, strode up to Hammond and embraced him in a bear hug.

"Maybe you could come back tomorrow."

"Tonight. We need it tonight."

"Sorry." But he made no effort at all to conceal the fact that he was *not* sorry.

"Please, we—"

"Look, I couldn't let you just walk out of here with a goddamn gas chromatograph, not without a written order. What the fuck's the matter with you? We only got two in the whole lab, and just one of those things costs—"

"Who *could* let me?"

"Nobody but the captain himself, and he—"

"Please call 'im."

"At 2:15 A.M.? You must be dumber—"

"I said 'please.'" With the gentleness of a parent lifting a child, Dominic Benedetto lifted the lab stool—with the suddenly terrified two-hundred-pound technician still sitting on it—and carried it easily to the telephone. Benedetto needed a gas chromatograph. It was on Hammond's list. Next he'd find an all-night market and get the aluminum foil.

———

Fasulo gave instructions to one of the junior officers, then turned back to Hammond, draped an arm around Hammond's shoulders, and led him to the rear of a truck, where the two sat together for twenty minutes. Sitting here under a giant pall of smoke, each man built a little fire to hold in his hand so he could draw smoke from it into his lungs. And they talked together about the big fire. Mostly Fasulo talked. Hammond asked questions and wrote a few words on a pad as Fasulo talked. Hammond would not interview any of the other firemen tonight. He might later, tomorrow or the day after, about some particular point, but he knew from experience that he would probably get his best information from the seasoned officer actively in charge. Others, even those who had walked inside the burning building, were concerned with bits and pieces of the problem, and they would probably not even agree with each other about the direction of the fire or the color of the smoke.

After leaving Fasulo, Hammond walked around the entire perimeter of the fire scene, so intent on details of the fire that he didn't recognize other firemen he knew, didn't see Hooker and Rosewater at work in the small clusters of onlookers in the night streets, didn't even notice the still-elegant black-and-white figure of Minot Winston Gault III, although he passed within feet of him, did not see Gault's smile.

Hammond judged that he had time to rest now, a little rest before the hours of work that lay ahead for him. He trudged the block back to "the office" and slumped on the back seat in the dark auto. Had Gault gone home to his bed now that he'd gotten *him* to work the night shift? That investigator whose place Hammond had taken, was he asleep? Maybe if he'd listened to Sheri Sue and not answered that goddamn phone— Sheri Sue; was she asleep now, in her own bed? If so, Hammond thought whimsically about her heartstopping young body, I'll bet she's sleeping on her *back*, and he smiled.

Hammond sat in the inky darkness and thought about Sheri Sue. Thought about her little-girl qualities. How she often walked with her chin held down to her neck, looking out at the world through wide-open eyes. How she would not drink water from a bathroom tap because it was different from the water available in the kitchen; she *knew* it was. How she made a large circle, a balloon, over the "i" when she wrote her name. How she would not even consider variety in sex. When she had first come to his home, she was so adoring and eager for him to be in her body that he was surprised when she flatly refused to take his penis in her mouth: "I don't *do* that." And he had found that anything else—anything other than the position she called The Right Way—was out. And he had yielded to her taboos. Because Sheri Sue could be more fun than Christmas morning. And in some ways, her little-girl immaturity was endearing.

Hammond did not want to do without Sheri Sue, but he was becoming increasingly uneasy about her nest-building proclivity. Why in hell do people feel that relationships have to go somewhere, that they necessarily have to *grow*—like a goddamn plant? And anyway, what's so wrong with getting a plant just the way you want it and then keeping it trimmed? Not every plant has to be a magic beanstalk. Hammond wanted a *limited* relationship with Sheri Sue. He had made that clear, hadn't he? It was what the two of them had *agreed* on. He had told her he would never marry again, had said it in just so many words. He had not led her on, was not using her. And yet Hammond felt a worm of doubt, felt perhaps just a little culpable—as any man might who does not reject the concept of love and who does not flatly refuse to believe that he himself might be lovable.

Hammond scrubbed a hand over his eyes to chase the doubt away and said aloud, "Aw, Christ." Using his jacket as a makeshift pillow, Hammond lay on the back seat, sort of. There wasn't room to stretch out, but he was too exhausted to care much about that.

Twenty minutes later, Hammond was falling down into the deepest stage of sleep when he was yanked cruelly back to consciousness by a paw agitating his recently abused arm and by "I'm back, Chieeeff. I'm back."

4

SMELLS

"IT's a good thing looks can't kill, Chieeeff."

"In your case, Benedetto, I think it might take a silver bullet to do the job."

Benedetto did not understand the reference, but he grinned.

Hammond tried to see the fire. Dark. Firemen still moving about, taking up hose. Hammond struggled out of the car and lighted a cigarette. He could not believe its taste, looked at the cigarette for an explanation, put it out.

"What time is it?" Hammond asked the question even though he wore a wristwatch. It was a means to redemonstrate his authority over Benedetto, and both men knew it.

"Three-fourteen, Chieeeff."

"Knock that off."

"Knock what off, Chieeeeeeff?"

BUSY said the large yellow letters on the panel truck. The letters leaned sharply to the right, and there were little horizontal lines coming off to the left to make it look as if the letters were zipping off to the right.

Smaller lettering underneath the *BUSY* explained the acronym: Board-Up Service for You.

Chicago makes a lot of work for board-up companies. More than forty of them. On short notice, they will nail sheathing or planks over doorways and other openings in a building to keep out weather, looters, vandals, winos, junkies, runaways, and hard-up lovers. And much of this work is done in the nighttime.

The *BUSY* truck was coming south on Elston, three blocks from the fire scene, when Sergeant Hooker spotted it. His hopes leaped. So far, his partner had not had much success at finding the building's owner and trying to get him down there. Several calls had turned up a name—Century Bank and Trust—but little more that would help. But maybe *BUSY* was on the way to the fire scene, called in by somebody representing the owner or tenant. Or maybe the driver had heard radio traffic about somebody who *was* called here. Hooker stepped out into the street and waved for the driver to pull up. The driver was startled and was reluctant to stop, but he saw the shield hung on the front of Hooker's suit coat, and he could hardly pretend he hadn't seen the officer's signal; the guy was standing right in his lane. He stopped and answered Hooker's questions: No, he was on his way to a call a couple of miles away; and no, he was sorry, but he didn't know a thing about Hooker's fire. Ah, well, shot in the dark, thought Hooker. He saw no reason to question the driver further, and it did not occur to him to record his name or license-plate number. He thanked the driver and waved him on. The driver returned his wave with a gloved hand.

———

The air was still damp-hot, even at three thirty-one in the morning, and Hammond was not eager to put on the coveralls that Benedetto had brought. Or the safety shoes. Or the battered hard hat which had been worn too many times before, by others.

"Couldn't you find a cruddier hat than this, Benedetto?"

"I doubt it, Chief."

"Finally, we agree on something."

However, there was no debate in Hammond's mind about whether to put on the protective gear. Few places are so black and feculent as a building just after it is ravaged by fire and wetted down with thousands of gallons of water. Or as treacherous; a burned-out building may be trembling in the balance, a killing pit.

While he was taking off his uniform and shoes and pulling on the protective clothing, Hammond recalled a movie scene that had amused him. The only film Hammond had ever seen about arson investigation was an English-made movie released in the early-1970s and that starred Chad Everett as a hotshot arson investigator in England. This hero and his comely blond aide are at a raging warehouse fire one night and decide to come back to investigate it the next day. And how do they dress for it? The hero shows up wearing a suede jacket and a dashing little scarf at his throat. No protective gear for this paladin. And his assistant investigator, this blond cupcake, walks into the fire scene wearing a pastel suit and white shoes and carrying a white handbag.

And will you look how *my* assistant looks, thought Hammond. How the goddamned Frankenstein monster would look if he were hit on the head till he was five feet high. And nine feet wide. Benedetto's coveralls lacked several inches of buttoning across his Brobdingnagian chest, but he showed no concern; he was not a man accustomed to getting a fit off the rack.

Hammond noticed with distaste that the leather band

inside his hard hat was stained, presumably greasy from previous wearings. He held the hat up to his nose and sniffed at the leather band.

Sid Ruck raised the book until it touched the tip of his nose. Then he inhaled, slowly, deeply, savoring the faint aroma of the leather binding. He remembered shoe stores that smelled ripe and agreeably pungent like this, and new leather gloves.

Ruck pressed the book gently against his cheek, and the deeply padded cover felt cool and soft, cool and soft like a woman's breast against his face.

The book gave no less pleasure to Ruck's eyes. The front cover was deeply inlaid with twenty-four-carat gold. The rag-linen pages were gilt edged, and a few of the pages had been embossed with impressive seals. The end sheets were of washed silk. Semitransparent fly sheets had elaborate leaf designs. There was even a bound-in leather ribbon to be used as a placemarker.

It had cost Ruck twelve thousand dollars to have this book written. Ruck thought the book was a pile of shit. Guano. Manure. Crap. And he loved it. And the book had encouraged him to do appalling violence.

Sid Ruck did not look at all like a violent man. Not this great soft bag of guts. Surely he must have to use whatever meager wits and energy he seemed to possess just to get that body through the day.

And in fact he *was* partly as he appeared to be. When he had flown to Florida seven years ago, he had had to travel in first class because he was too fat to fit into a tourist-class seat. And since his arrival here on Sundown Key, he had gotten horrified attention by spitting in lobbies and in elevators.

But Ruck was not poor. His suite here was running almost three hundred dollars a day. And although no public records showed it, Ruck was the effective owner of more than one hundred buildings in Chicago.

And he was not stupid. Ruck knew old buildings in much the same way that a knacker knows old farm animals. He knew how much an old building could be bought for, how much it could be sold for, how much it could be insured for. Ruck could quote, from memory, any passage from the standard 165-line fire policy:

> ... This entire policy shall be void if, whether before or after a loss, the insured has willfully concealed or misrepresented any material fact or circumstance concerning this insurance or the subject thereof, or the interest of the insured therein, or in cases of any fraud or false swearing ...

And Ruck was not lazy. Hours past bedtime, the fat man was rereading a three-hundred-and-fifty-seven-page report, an insurance appraisal report with a padded leather cover on the outside that smelled like new shoes and with several signatures on the inside that attested to the opinion that a certain three-story warehouse on Clybourn Street in Chicago, Illinois, was worth two million, four hundred and thirty thousand dollars. Ruck knew that he couldn't have sold that warehouse for more than seven hundred and fifty thousand, not even when the appraisal was new. So what? The important thing was that an insurance company had accepted the appraisal. Did *they* believe it? Maybe. Maybe not. The premiums on a two-million-dollar policy on an old warehouse in Chicago are a hell of a lot of dollars.

And certainly Sid Ruck was not without his dreams and ambitions. This very night he hoped to effect a "sale" of that warehouse, for two or three times its value, to an insurance company.

And there were going to be other nights.

Ruck was feeling godlike. He made stories up and then real people acted them out in their real lives, mostly people who were quite unaware of his existence. In fact, although Ruck's secret business had given at least part-time employment to dozens and had brought unwelcome drama to hundreds, there were just two people on this earth who knew Sid Ruck was involved. One of the two was Ruck's cat's-paw, a young man whom Ruck regarded as a little bughouse but absolutely loyal. No problem there.

The other guy who knew, well, that was a very different story. The sonofabitch had stumbled across one of Ruck's incendiary activities before Ruck had finished erecting a mountain of obfuscation around himself. Dead-bang he'd had Ruck. Hot and cold and up, down, and sideways. Just thinking of that time could still do unpleasant things to Ruck's huge belly. Ruck had offered the man money, lots of money, not believing he'd take it. Guy was a real goody-goody, straight-arrow type. Knowing the sonofabitch would never agree. Straight Arrow agreed. With stupendous relief that put bubbles in his blood, Ruck bought his way out—literally with a suitcaseful of cash. And before it was over, it had gotten even sweeter. Sid Ruck had three photographs now, one of a battered suitcase closed, one of the same suitcase open and full of cash, and one of guess who walking away from the camera carrying guess what. A grainy thing, that third picture, taken with an 8x lens; no work of art, but you could tell who it was, all right, if you already knew. Gotcha! Your proofs'll be ready Tuesday, Straight Arrow. Later, Ruck had mailed a copy of the third photo to the guy's home; let *him* know how it feels to be grabbed by the balls. Gotcha, Straight Arrow! Guy was still a trusted minion of the great City of Chicago, and he couldn't hurt Ruck without going down too. It reminded Ruck of an old joke: This lady goes into the dentist's office, gets up into his chair, and just before he starts in on her, she reaches over and grabs his balls in a powerful grip and says to him, ever so sweetly, "Now, we're not going to hurt each other, are we?" Sid Ruck reached out and caught an imaginary pair of balls in a vicious grip, and he grinned and said ever so sweetly, "Now, we're not going to hurt each other, are we, Straight Arrow?"

5

MONKEY BUSINESS

DOMINIC Benedetto had one mother of an hour. It began with Hammond and his big loudmouthed crony, Fasulo, deciding that—since most of the first floor was buried under debris and since it wasn't safe to walk up onto the second or third floors or the roof—they'd have their first look over the burned-out building from the outside, from an aerial platform. Benedetto felt panic taking his body: His stomach made a fist, his legs began to tremble. How could he tell them, Hammond and Fasulo, that he had a terror of heights, that he was afraid to go up there in the sky, to go up in a bucket on the end of some poles with a lot of joints that were going to break or bend the wrong way. Look, I'm not afraid to risk dying, but I can't—*what?* Either you *feel* the terror or you don't understand it, and Benedetto knew that Hammond and Fasulo had never felt this; firemen were all a pack of goddamned monkeys, just as happy swinging by their tails as they were standing on the ground. When the time came, Benedetto stepped into the basket, saying nothing, knowing he was going to die. And up they went—the three of them, rub-a-dub-dub—into space, just three men and fifty bats up there for thirty minutes that seemed to Dominic Benedetto to last half his lifetime. With each tremble and lurch of the basket,

Benedetto had closed his eyes, held his breath, and strangled the railing. But Hammond and Fasulo didn't even hold on; Fasulo worked the spotlights, directed movements of the bucket, and offered a few jokes; Hammond even wrote in his notebook while the bucket was moving. Benedetto regarded them with a pure-white hatred born of his fear. Monkeys, that's what they are, fuckin' monkeys; put a monkey on this contraption and it probably wouldn't mind a bit, but try to give a *lion* a ride on this thing and its mane would fall out. If I threw these monkeys out of here, he reasoned, they'd have to put this thing back on the ground; almost be worth the maximum penalty for monkey murder. The hating was something to focus on, but only between movements of the gondola, and there were enough movements to age a man who suffered from acrophobia. The hair at the base of Benedetto's skull stayed wet, fear-wet, and it felt cold despite the warmth of the air. When he stepped back onto the ground at last, Benedetto had trouble walking. He ached for a rest but he was not to get it. It took Hammond only one minute to give two Fire Department guards their orders: Rope off the block and prevent anyone from entering the fire scene without his personal order, no matter who wanted in, no matter what it took to stop them. Hammond spent a second minute saying good-bye to Fasulo, a third minute giving instructions to the photographer, and two more minutes talking with Hooker and Rosewater. Benedetto recognized that Hammond was running the whole show, with no competition from him. Just give me some rest, Benedetto thought; give me some time and *then* we'll see, see how monkeys do when *they're* under pressure. But there had been no more time, no more rest for Benedetto, just those five minutes to get back some dominion over his own legs; then in they tramped, just Hammond and Benedetto, to inspect the ground floor. It had been a lopsided contest. Hammond instructed Benedetto not to talk unless he saw something important; Benedetto wasn't clear on what he was looking for. Hammond was inured to the Stygian blackness of a fire scene at night, knew how to move over the treacherous landscape; Benedetto was on an alien planet. Hammond carried only a flashlight and notebook, so his hands were free to make notes, which he did often; Benedetto, in the role of flunkey, carried a flashlight, a rack of floodlights, a pole with a hook near one end, and a hydrocarbon detector. The weight of this gear was no burden for the powerful Benedetto, but carrying it prevented him from using his arms for balance, and he fell twice, kaflopped down into the vile rubbish, and Hammond laughed at him. As Benedetto braced himself to get up after the second fall, his left hand felt something that was strangely *smooth*. He looked to see what it was—a *face*—and snatched his hand away. It was the head of a doll. "What the hell is *that* doing in here?" Benedetto said, and Hammond laughed again.

One more laugh, one more laugh ought to just about do it, thought Benedetto; there are plenty of places to hide a body in here.

6

NIGHT SCHOOL

"LET's see your brights," ordered Hammond.

Benedetto switched off his flashlight and gave it a vigorous shove into the pocket of his coveralls. The ill-fitting coveralls channeled the thrust right into his crotch. Reacting to sudden pain in his right testis, Benedetto crouched forward and dropped the portable floodlights. An umbrella of gray dust formed in the air over the light bar and began to fall apart.

"Now what?"

"Nothin'. Everythin' is *perfect*." Benedetto's tone promised violence if Hammond tried to proceed with this conversation. He had endured a full hour of torture now and he was looking for an end to it.

Benedetto switched on the "brights." The portable floodlights showed them a scene that was difficult for Benedetto to comprehend. Surrealistic, black on black. Shadows slid eerily around unrecognizable objects as the beam moved over them.

Roughly in the middle of the ground floor of the mutilated corpse of the warehouse, the two men stood before an enclosure of some sort. An office? Rest room? Blackened frame walls. Charred wood door, ajar. A rectangular opening in the top half of the door had obviously been a window; there were still fragments of glass along the bottom edge of the opening. Through this opening, they could make out a desk and chairs under a snowfall of gray debris; the enclosure had been a one-room office.

"Shine the light down here. No, don't move. Don't take a step you don't have to until I get a chance to check the glass on the floor. Hold it *still*."

Hammond studied the outer surface of the door and the wall nearby, his face so close at times that his nose almost touched the wall. Then he sat down on the floor, gingerly, concerned that sharp objects might be hidden underneath and not wanting to send dry ashes billowing into the air. Using the edge of a clipboard as a blade, Hammond gently scraped a half-inch-deep layer off the top of a patch of ashes that lay along the outside of the office wall near the door. He repeated this act again and again, pausing now and then to examine bits of debris. This went on until Hammond had bared wooden flooring at the base of the office wall. Then the drillmaster shifted onto his hands and knees and put his head down close to the flooring, moving his nose slowly along the baseboard and sniffing.

Like a goddamned rat terrier, thought Benedetto; I run my ass off gettin' equipment together and put up with all kinds of bullshit so I can come in here and see this schoolmarm do his magic, and what happens? The sonofabitch just roots around in the crap like a goddamned rat terrier while I stand here pretendin' I'm a fuckin' lamppost.

"Hold the light still," said Hammond, as to a slow child.

"How'd you like—"

"Go get our gear in here, all of it. And bring the photographer with you. Tell him to bring all *his* stuff."

While Benedetto was gone, Hammond sat back down

in the filth, held his flashlight in his mouth, and wrote in his notebook. Benedetto was back in minutes, bringing the photographer, Breedlove, with him, both men loaded down with equipment and finding it difficult to keep their balance. Hammond rose and motioned absently for them to set the gear down. The drillmaster was grappling with a question that seemed to have only two possible answers, both of which were wrong: Do I try to keep control of a Neanderthal like Benedetto by keeping him in the dark, or do I train him up so that he'll be more useful—and more of a threat to me? Lovely choice, thought Hammond. Just lovely.

———

"Yeah?"

"Mr. King, please."

"Who's calling?"

"Uh, this is Mr. Messenger. Is that you, sir?"

"Yeah. Anything new there?"

"I have some bad news for you."

"Tell me."

"Your dog, he got sick and died."

"Hunh. When?"

"He got this attack, really terrible, about midnight our time."

"Did he suffer long?"

"Two, three hours. They did everything they knew how, but they never had a chance of saving him."

"Are you sure? That he's *dead*?"

"I saw the body."

"You're a good man. You *will* take care of the rest of the litter, won't you?"

On Sundown Key, the man who answered to the name of King stood outside a phone booth because he was too fat to squeeze inside. He reached into the booth and hung up. He had not placed the call, but he inserted two fingers into the coin-return recess to explore for forgotten coins. Nothing. On impulse, the man leaned over, spat noisily into his hand, then tucked the viscous glob under the hinged cover, into the coin-return recess. He chuckled: The next person who slipped fingers in there *would* find something.

In Chicago, the man calling himself Mr. Messenger replaced the receiver with a gloved hand.

The black bowels of the warehouse became a bizarre classroom. With Breedlove holding lights, Hammond laid a hand on the mutilated surface of the office wall and spoke to Benedetto.

"A blistered surface like this looks sort of like an alligator's hide—you see?—so the pattern is called alligatoring. And the pattern of alligatoring each time tells us something about the fire that made it. In this case, you see fat blisters in a rhythmic pattern; you see a faint sheen; and you see these deep crimp marks between the blisters. These are the tracks of a hot fire, a *fast* fire. In a slow, not-so-hot fire, the blisters are flat, and the crimp marks between them don't go very deep."

As he spoke, Hammond reverted to the quintessential teacher. Benedetto was nodding his buffalo head, the absorbed student.

. Hammond squatted down where he had earlier cleared ashes and debris away from the base of the wall. "Now, look how the wall is charred all the way down, right down to the floor. And the charring down here is very heavy, maybe heavier than up there at the ceiling. Well, that's not normal. Fire burns *up*, if it can, and the temperature at the floor is usually only about one third as hot as it is at the ceiling, less than a third—maybe three hundred to five hundred degrees at the floor, maybe sixteen hundred degrees at the ceiling. There's no basement here, and on the lowest floor, the bottom edge of a wall is hard to burn because it doesn't get air very well. On the other hand, if you pour a flammable liquid on the floor, right up to the wall, you're going to get this kind of a burn pattern. You may even see the fire eat right under the baseboard if the accelerant seeps in under there."

Hammond told Breedlove to take photographs of the lower wall and the baseboard. While Breedlove labored with lights, angle, focus, lens opening, and speed, Hammond pried sections of the baseboard away with a wrecking bar and found charring inside. Even the bottom face of the baseboard was blackened.

Hammond chose a three-inch-long piece of the baseboard to keep as an exhibit and put it into a bottle. He twisted a cap on, made it tight. On an evidence tag, he printed the address, the date, the time, and a designation for this first exhibit: A. He signed the tag and had Benedetto sign it. He made a loop of the two loose ends of the string on the evidence tag by knotting them tightly together. Then he cut a length of adhesive tape, passed it through the loop, and used it to seal the edge of the cap of the evidence bottle, making sure that the knot was between the tape and the bottle and that the ends of the tape overlapped. Hammond licked a gummed paper sticker, stuck it across the tape overlap, and initialed the sticker. Finally, he recorded the exhibit in his notebook, noting where he had found it and who was with him at the time.

While he went through this ritual handling of the exhibit, Hammond talked quietly. "This was arson, all right, but good arson cases are kicked away every day by arson investigators who quit working at the fire scene before they're done. You don't quit until you can show that your explanation is the only one that fits. You don't settle for one piece of evidence if five pieces of evidence would get you farther. Or *fifty*. And the way you preserve your evidence at the fire scene can make you look like a wonder worker or a nincompoop. You use only absolutely clean containers that won't let fumes pass in or out. You use the smallest container that will hold an object. And you prepare yourself to prove—maybe a year, two years later—that nobody could have tampered with your evidence."

By the time Hammond was performing his ritual on Exhibit H (a chunk of the office door wrapped up in aluminum foil), Dominic Benedetto's vocabulary had grown to include "spalling," "crazing," and "demarkation," and he had seen how it is possible for an expert— even in a wasteland of crap like this—to read the tracks of a fire. Like an Indian guide recognizing day-old bear turds. Except that Hammond paid attention to burn patterns, to what melted and what didn't melt, to colors, to accumulations of soot, and to what lay on top of what on the floor. Cute act, thought Benedetto.

In the quiet of the dark, ruined building, Benedetto and Breedlove listened to the three-story-high corpse make sounds as its heat-distended pieces cooled and as water that had been pumped onto upper floors worked its way downward. The sounds told them to run, to get out of here fast before the building collapsed on them; Benedetto and Breedlove stood there watching Hammond, hoping he was listening to the sounds too.

The drillmaster worked the tip of a wrecking bar under the wooden sill laid in the office doorway, levering the sill up in stages until most of it came free in one piece. He turned the three-foot-long chunk of wood over, saw that the underside had been savagely attacked by fire, and felt a surge of pleasure. He handed the sill to Breedlove. "Don't let anything happen to that. Just hold it."

"Yes, sir."

The sill and the wooden flooring abutting it had been laid over a concrete slab. Hammond put his face down where the sill had been and sniffed along the trough. Then he made careful readings with the vapor detector and recorded the numbers in his notebook. He used a wood chisel and a hammer to chip off pieces of the subflooring along the sill trough, and he put pungent-smelling chips into two small jars. Crouching down low over the sill trough, Hammond used a flashlight to soften the shadows that escaped the floodlights. "Have a look at this," he said to Benedetto.

As the policeman moved down close, like a grizzly bear coming down onto all fours, he came between the floodlights and the sill trough, blocking out most of the light.

"A total eclipse!" snapped Hammond.

Benedetto scuttled to the other side of the sill trough, next to Hammond.

"These cracks in the slab, it looks like they go all the way around that piece," the drillmaster said. "Or just about. See? I wonder what it would take to get that piece out. Maybe if we brought an air hammer in here—"

"I can take it out." Benedetto said it quietly, as a fact.

Hammond looked at Benedetto's broad face and remembered this thug yanking him through the air with one hand. Well, Hammond thought, he'd either fail or he'd open up the floor. Hammond shrugged and told him, "Then do it."

Benedetto shoved the tapered end of a long wrecking

bar into the crack and hit the blunt end of it with the side of a heavy hammer head, hard. Then he took hold of the bar and heaved his body mass backward. The floor cried out at the force of the violation, and Benedetto kept going, right over backward, into a pratfall with his feet high in the air and a cloud of ashes swirling up around him. Startled, Breedlove stepped backward, tripped, and fell down heavily, but he held onto the sill that Hammond had given him to hold. Lying flat on his back, Breedlove held up the sill as if it were a game-winning ball he had just caught in the end zone.

"Jesus, the kind of help you get these days!" said Hammond, but he was grinning.

It took another twenty minutes of steady work to scoop damp earth from the gap in the concrete subfloor into two jars ("one for the lab and one for us"), to make more readings with the hydrocarbon-vapor detector and record them (high positive), to saw the tip off a wooden desk leg (charred on the bottom), and to finish recording the exhibits (now through Exhibit L).

"We'll take this evidence out now and seal it in a drum," said Hammond. "And take a break, get some coffee. But leave all the gear here."

"We got more to do in here?" Benedetto asked. "Yet tonight?"

The night air moved slowly because it was carrying a heavy load: the dungy-smelling exhalations of the swampy region southeast of Chicago. In summer, that southeast wind can be an evil thing.

Eldert Maddox also moved slowly. He was tired, but he was reluctant to let the night end. He carried a paper cup of coffee back to his truck, sat on the front seat, sipped the scalding coffee, and thought about the future.

Three down, fourteen to go.

Fourteen more nights like this.

Unless somebody saw the pattern—and there was a chance of that—and was waiting for him. Waiting for him at one of those fourteen buildings. Waiting for him on one of those fourteen nights.

And then it came to him: Why not *one* night? Why not burn all fourteen buildings in one night?

That would be nuts, wouldn't it? Eleven of the fourteen buildings were right by the one he had burned tonight. Which was riskier? Burning the eleven buildings which still stood in that neighborhood on *eleven* nights, or taking them all out in *one* night? One big, bright night. Eldert was excited by the idea, and in some ways it made a hell of a lot of sense.

How do you burn down eleven buildings in the same neighborhood on the same night? Lots of ways. Yeah, but here's the question: How do you make it look like it wasn't for the insurance? An accident—like the fire was caused by faulty wiring or spontaneous combustion? No way. That's fine for just one building, but not for *eleven*. You want each building to be a total loss, and you wouldn't get that job done by setting one fire and hoping it spread to ten more buildings. If you want eleven total losses, you build eleven separate fires. Or twenty-two or forty-four. And if you do that, it's obvious it's arson for the insurance, right? Well, maybe, maybe not. What if you burned down a lot of the neighboring buildings too, made it look like some maniac was trying to burn down *all* the buildings in that area instead of just *certain* buildings? How many more buildings would that take? A dozen? Two dozen'd be more convincing. Don't forget about the other three buildings, southeast.

And some neighboring buildings to make that look good too?

Fifty buildings?

Setting good fires takes time. And you need access. How could you set good fires in that many buildings and get away? A few minutes later, Eldert Maddox thought he had the answer.

7

SILHOUETTES

HAMMOND came half awake in a dimly lit room, lacking the will to pull his mind into needle-sharp focus. He brought a hand up to explore, carefully. Something over his right ear, soft and bulky—a bandage. Tender, swollen area across the back of his skull. He rolled his head carefully to the left and saw a siderail, realized he was in a hospital bed. He touched his neck, then his chest, abdomen, groin. No damage apparent. He worked the fingers of each hand and then held his arms up. Soreness in one arm called up an ugly memory of Benedetto yanking him around in the street outside the command bus. Hammond tried moving his feet, sensed at once that there was something wrong with his left foot, or leg. He lay still and closed his eyes, thinking back. He remembered the fire. Gault. Benedetto. Aerial platform. Inside that warehouse. Coming out. Sealing the samples in a drum. Then they sat down outside and drank hot coffee. And then—and then—*nothing*. Hammond groped for a call button.

From where he stood on Elston Avenue, Eldert Maddox could see a sign that said CLOSED. The sign was machine-lettered on cardboard, and it hung in a window, fastened onto the little ring at the bottom of the window shade. What made it interesting was that the sign hung between lace curtains in a second-floor, walk-up room over a store. Pull the shade down, "doctor" is in. Prostitute? Numbers? Somebody selling horse tranquilizer? The customers would know. Eldert assumed the police wouldn't care, not here.

He regarded this as yet another proof of his conviction that Chicago had too many worm-eaten people in too many worm-eaten neighborhoods. As if more proof were needed, he thought. He had already seen enough of that this afternoon. Eight-year-olds with cigarettes stuck in their faces. Frame houses that had even worse posture than the old people who half lived in them. A pack of boys throwing a baseball back and forth over all the lanes of North Street traffic without a thought about the risk to drivers, pedestrians, and store windows—or, more likely, it was that very risk that made the activity appealing to them. Bars, bars, bars. For-sale and for-rent signs that looked as senile as the buildings they offered, as if the signs had been nailed on the buildings back when they were new and never taken down.

Eldert wore nondescript clothes, work shoes, a cap, dark glasses, and work gloves. His jaw was beginning to ache from holding a pipe he never lit. Very little of Eldert showed; if people should be questioned at some future time about any strangers hanging around, they wouldn't be likely to recall much about what *he* looked like.

Eldert had been on foot for almost six hours now. Avoiding only the scene of last night's fire, he had made a walking tour of a large area on both sides of the North Branch of the river. The bold concept that had galvanized him last night had looked like merely a pipe dream during his first hour on the streets today. Then, by steps he could not perceive, his attitude had begun to change. And a conviction formed and case-hardened: It *could* be done. It would take study, planning, work— Eldert began to walk again, enjoying a high. The neighborhood was painfully hot. But not, thought Eldert, like it's *going* to be.

———————

It was as if Robert Hammond were the grand marshal and his pushing the call button had been the signal to start a parade. First a nurse. There was an instant as she moved through the doorway when she became a silhouette that made Hammond think of a flagpole, then she became a nurse again. She frowned and hesitated when he asked for a cigarette; but when she finally acceded, she put one of Hammond's cigarettes between her own lips and lit it for him, handling it like an experienced smoker. In answer to his questions, she told him it was almost four o'clock—yes, on Tuesday; yes, four o'clock in the afternoon on Tuesday—and that he had been brought to her floor at about five o'clock Tuesday morning. She told him that Mr. Gault was in the hospital and had asked to be notified when Hammond awoke. It was obvious from her manner that she did not regard Gault as a routine hospital visitor.

However, it was a staff doctor who marched second silhouette in the parade. He gave what seemed to Hammond to be oblique answers to his questions, but the doctor did manage to convey the information. Hammond had received a heavy blow on the head, but X-rays had revealed no fractures of the skull. A flap of flesh had been gouged almost off the side of his head and had hung down over his ear, but that had been stitched back into place. The doctor preferred not to give Hammond any medications for pain because he didn't believe in masking symptoms in cases involving head injuries. A bone in the left ankle had been cracked, so a temporary cast was put on, and corrective surgery was scheduled for midmorning tomorrow. Hammond would possibly feel drowsy, lethargic for a couple of days, but that shouldn't pose any problem here, should it? Oh, yes, it's quite common to lose recall of events that took place just before a heavy blow on the head, very ordinary, nothing to worry about at all. No, we don't know just yet how long you'll need to be here; we'll know better in a couple of days; meantime, you might just as well settle in comfortably.

And Gault was next. Minot Winston Gault III, elegant in a summer-thin dove-gray suit, crisp white shirt, and wine-colored necktie. He sat on a chair beside Hammond's bed and crossed his legs, and as he talked and shifted in the chair, his trouser cuffs worked up, and it was obvious that his black hose were amazingly long. Hammond wondered whimsically if the hose went all the way up to Gault's self-certified balls. In addition to being fire commissioner and a close political ally of the mayor, Gault sat on numerous boards, at least two of which had some effect on the funding of this hospital, so he was deferred to; he had already been copiously informed about Hammond's condition. Hammond told Gault that he couldn't remember what had happened after he had sealed the evidence in a drum and had a cup of coffee. Gault made a small joke about drinking better coffee, then told Hammond that he had gone back inside the burned-out warehouse and that part of the building had fallen in on him.

"What about—what's his name?"

"Benedetto. He's here too."

"And Breedlove—"

"Stayed outside."

"Then Benedetto and I were the only ones in there?"

"Right."

"Is Benedetto okay?"

"Not too bad. They strapped a shoulder up, put a cast on one arm."

"I assume they had to bring in a veterinarian for *that*. You know, Mo, I never wanted the goddamned job, wouldn't want it now, but at the same time, I hate the idea of losing anything to that—"

"Rob, he wasn't hurt in the cave-in. Not according to what Breedlove tells us. He was hurt pulling stuff off of *you*. Breedlove thinks you would have bought it if Benedetto hadn't been there."

Hammond opened his mouth to speak but didn't. He lit a cigarette but laid it in a little steel pan and forgot to smoke it. Gault sat quietly, waiting for Hammond. When the drillmaster did speak, it was not about Benedetto.

"The evidence safe?"

"Locked up."

"And my notebook?"

"Yes."

"Do we still have the fire scene?"

"Umhmm. Guards are still there, and Kleinschmidt says we can hang onto it for a while."

Hammond assured Gault that his memory of events at the fire scene, at least through the time he had sealed the evidence, was lucid and that, if they could ever bring anybody to trial, he could support a contention of arson in a dozen different ways.

Gault smiled warmly and said, "*Your* part of this case I'm not going to worry about, Rob. I only hope Benedetto or whoever takes over from here does half the job you've done, my boy." He shook Hammond's hand. "I'll look in on you in the morning if you don't mind. In the meantime, if there's anything—"

"There is one thing, Mo."

"Name it."

"Will you ask him to stop and see me before he leaves?"

She threw her arms wide and the packages spilled out and her words spilled out like the packages: how worried she had been when he hadn't answered her phone calls this morning, how the worry had turned to fear when he didn't appear at the Academy as usual, and how she had wept—just sat at her desk and bawled—when word was passed at the Academy that he had been injured but would be all right. She pulled the chair close to his bed, held his arm with both of her hands, and began to tell him, in copious detail, of the laudatory remarks about him at the Academy.

To change the subject, Hammond asked what was in all the packages.

She opened each sack and box and showed him the contents: puzzles, magazines, nuts, and chewing gum for him; magazines and snacks for her. She asked him please, couldn't they have a TV set put in? As she chattered on with high animation, it became clear to Hammond that Sheri Sue was elated at the prospect of having him to herself for several hours a day.

Hammond felt captive. He did not want her practically to *move in* with him. He spoke to her of having surgery in the morning, of quiet and rest, of reports to be written, of visits by fire and police officials. He told her that he would miss her and that he would call her in a few days when he felt better.

Sheri Sue's teary protest was interrupted by a knock on the half-closed door to Hammond's room.

Preemptively, Sheri Sue said, "Yes?"

The door was swung open far enough for a nurse to lean in. It wasn't the Flagpole; this one was shaped more like a shrub. A glance at Sheri Sue's face told her she was interrupting an emotional scene. "I'll come back later," she said softly and didn't wait for a response.

Unsure of how to proceed with her beloved Hammond, Sheri Sue resorted to what she considered her best strength. She pushed the door shut and walked slowly back to his bed with an exaggerated deliberateness that said: Here I come, and nothing can stop me. She lifted his hand in both of hers, kissed it, and guided it to her breast. Of course Hammond had noticed that Sheri Sue was braless under her blouse; on Sheri Sue, the effect was as unsubtle as the headlamps on a Bugatti. With a girlish giggle, she told him that she had decided to make it easier for him. He held her and gave her breasts reverential attention. He told her that the great icons of the City of Chicago came in *twos*: the bronze lions in front of the Art Institute, the twin Marina Towers, and her two breasts. "You go home, Sheri Sue, and if the whole city catches fire"—he milked her huge breasts vigorously and made a squirting noise by blowing air through his teeth—"I'll know just where to come to get the equipment that'll save us all."

"Nope. I'm going to stay here. Forever."

"Forever, eh? Well, that would give you time to do something very, very nice for me."

With a hand behind her neck he drew her face slowly down toward a teepee in the middle of his sheet. He felt her sudden resistance, increased the pull. She tore loose with more force than needed, marched to the door, yanked it open, and strode out looking straight ahead.

Hammond lit a cigarette and pushed out the smoke in a visible sigh. Why in the hell did he make the same bonehead mistakes over and over again?

The Shrub came through the doorway. Swiftly, he drew his good leg up under the sheet to make a teepee taller than the one made by his erection, too late he was sure. Her grin, he thought, looked—kind.

"You want to get a back rub or anything?"

"Uh, no, thanks."

8

AFTER DARK

WHATEVER the thing is, it keeps its back to a thirty-one-story-high civic building. An enormous bird of prey? A winged horse? The great head of a woman? Some have offered the opinion that it's a joke on Chicago and that its designer, Pablo Picasso, died with a smile on his lips. Fact is, nobody is quite sure *what* the hell it is. But there it stands, on all three shifts, guarding Daley Plaza. Maybe this curiously crude juju of a great city is the perfect reminder of Richard J. Daley. It's a oner. Praised and damned. Durable. The focus of a local government that dwarfs the man in the street.

One of the buildings overlooking Daley Plaza and the Picasso creature is a dirty old fortress called the City Hall-County Building. Twelve stories of limestone and marble. Actually, it's *two* structures, which—though delivered four years apart—are identical: Siamese twins joined at various floors.

Every day fire takes another shot at Chicago, and no building is immune, not even this one. One day City Hall caught fire. Five alarms. Twenty-four engine companies battled the fire. Meanwhile, up on the sixth floor, the men in the Fire Department's main communications room were breathing the smoke but they kept right on handling responses to *this* fire and to other fires. By luck and good work, a major disaster was averted.

That was years ago. And officials learned a lesson, right? They *did* install sprinklers, didn't they? And move the communications center to a safer location? And take adequate measures to protect Chicago's and Cook County's records? And get rid of all the major fire hazards?

Nah.

Lights burned in Room 105 on the City Hall side. Fire Commissioner Minot Winston Gault III sat at his desk and talked to a man who stood behind him, leaning over to study something on Gault's desk. The visitor had a dark suit, carefully combed hair, and intelligent eyes in a face that should have been on a prize fighter, the kind they call a trial horse. He could have been considered rather handsome for a rugged man were it not for the fact that the left side of his face had been crushed and not made just right again.

Moments before, Gault had opened a large envelope that lay on his desk and withdrawn a stack of glossy photographs. With a sweep of his hand, he spread them and chose four to show to the visitor.

Gault said, "A Fire Department photographer, man named Breedlove, took these last night. These last four he took after the cave-in. Besides Chief Hammond, the only man in the warehouse at the time of the cave-in was a police lieutenant named Benedetto. Do you know him?"

"*Dominic* Benedetto," said the visitor, but that was all he said. In his line of work, one tried not to volunteer information.

Gault chose words carefully now and spoke softly. "This matter is very delicate. That is why I asked you to come here so late. Any burned-out building can collapse at any time, but in this case, the cave-in was very *localized,* and the post that was holding up the stuff that fell on Chief Hammond"—Gault tapped a forefinger on one of the photographs of the fire scene—"the supporting post broke here—you see?—and, well, I think your people are the experts in such things, and I know you have outside specialists on tap."

"You're saying the cave-in was *caused?*"

"I'm asking you what *you* think."

"Commissioner, let me ask a few questions."

Gault nodded.

"Lieutenant Benedetto, he was *not* hurt?"

"Well, they tell me he wasn't hurt in the cave-in. As the others came running into the building after the noise, it looked to them like Benedetto might be pulling stuff off of Chief Hammond and some of it shifted onto *him.* Broke an arm, did something to his shoulder."

"I see," said the visitor, as if he were reluctant to let go of the second word. "Uh, Commissioner, are you familiar with Lieutenant Benedetto's history?"

"Not really, Captain. I know only that there was a fuss over there a few years ago that involved him, shake-up of some kind. Now some people—some policemen—would rather associate with a rattlesnake."

The man with the broken face was thoughtful, made no response.

Gault said, "I want this as confidential as possible, Captain."

"I understand, of course," the policeman said. "I'll need technical help, but we'll keep the cast as small as we can and be damned careful who's in it. I'd like a set of those photos, sir."

"Take these."

"Do you still have the fire scene?"

"Yes. I'll have our guards instructed to admit you and any people you designate. Do you know when you'll want to begin?"

"Yes, sir. Soon as the sun comes up."

———————————

Hammond awakened. Except for faint light issuing from somewhere below his bed, there was blackness. He lay still and tried on bittersweet memories, like a boy testing the exquisite soreness after a tooth came out.

He thought about his former wife and about Suzanne. The infant Suzanne, who took her thumb out of her mouth and offered it to Hammond. The toddler Suzanne who brought him magazines endlessly and announced, "MAZageens." The seven-year-old Suzanne who caressed the hair on Hammond's forearms and looked right inside his eyes as only—

With the suddenness of an electric shock, Hammond sensed something near his left side. He reacted with an involuntary lurch. There in the dark, so close that Hammond could have reached out and touched him, stood the massive silhouette of Dominic Benedetto. Hammond pulled himself up jerkily and switched on an adjustable lamp fastened to his bed. In its light, he got a better look at the policeman. Benedetto wore slippers, pajama bottoms, and a faded red robe with the left sleeve tucked under the belt, empty. His left arm was in a sling, and the shoulder was covered by a webwork of tape. The tape looked snowy against his dark skin.

"What time is it?" Hammond said. "What the hell are you *doing* here?"

That too-deep voice answered, "Commissioner Gault asked me to see you."

Because Hammond was embarrassed about having

been scared, he said, "It's just that I'm not used to having you be the first thing I see in the morning."

Benedetto made no response.

Hammond motioned toward the chair. Benedetto ignored the gesture. It was quiet for long seconds, and they heard somebody walk by in the hall.

Hammond lit a cigarette, let the smoke out slowly, and said, "The reason I asked to see you—what you did—"

Benedetto looked down and said, as if addressing his own feet, "Look, forget that crap." Clearly, he was uncomfortable. Then: "Anything else on yer mind?"

"Well, yes there is," Hammond said. "We didn't get started off just right, uh, working together, but there's no reason we *couldn't*. I'd like to try. I may not be moving around too swiftly, but I do know arson, and I think I could help you. We could talk about it."

Benedetto said nothing.

The silence grew awkward. Hammond added, "You want to?"

Benedetto's eyes closed and his buffalo head fell back and he laughed, derisively. "Right now," he told Hammond, "you're about as much good as a broken dick." Benedetto clumped out of the room, and Hammond could hear him out in hall, still laughing.

The two men sat at a table and waited. The coffee shop in the basement of the hospital had a seven-foot ceiling, which was painted brown; it had concrete pillars a man couldn't reach around. Twenty-four-year-old Sergeant Dennis Rosewater thought he could, some-how, feel the thousands of tons of hospital pressing down. Forty-nine-year-old Sergeant Vernon Hooker wanted to be home in bed.

But when he spotted Lieutenant Dominic Benedetto walking toward them, Hooker tucked his hands up into his armpits; flapped his elbows up and down; and, as if this aerodynamic monstrosity were efficacious, rose a few inches off his chair—this by way of providing illustration to what he said to the approaching Benedetto: "Behold! The phoenix has risen from the ashes!"

Benedetto responded by looking slightly pained and saying, "Psychiatric ward's up on eight, Hooks." Benedetto didn't know exactly what the phoenix reference meant, and it momentarily stirred a feeling that pained him often: that other people seemed to know a lot of stuff he didn't.

The two detective sergeants had taken only a few hours' sleep Tuesday morning and then returned to work. Vernon Hooker now had a list of owners to match the vehicles parked near the fire scene and had rewritten his notes on people he had questioned nearby. Meanwhile, Dennis Rosewater, in a telephone call to Century Bank and Trust Company, had learned two things: title to the Clybourn Street warehouse was held by the bank's trust department, and the property was under lease to Second City Wholesalers, Inc. "They sell toys and specialty stuff to big department stores and such," Rosewater said. And Benedetto remembered yanking his hand away from a doll's head lying in the crap at the fire scene, then remembered Hammond laughing at him. Tuesday afternoon, Hooker had made a preliminary check on Second City's credit standing (strong); and Rosewater had met with Second City owners, who said they couldn't see any motive for a deliberate fire.

"They haven't had lawsuits or labor problems lately," Rosewater reported. "Nobody with a real hard-on for 'em they can think of, and there wasn't much merchandise in the building yet. They just took the building three, four weeks ago. Beginning to stock up for Christmas."

"Christmas?!" said Benedetto.

"That's what *I* said," Rosewater said. "Hard to think of Christmas in July."

A layer of lemon gelatin lay over the moon. Robert Hammond braced his elbows on the windowsill and peered out. He hadn't asked for permission to crawl out of bed; it would most probably have been refused. He pressed his forehead against the glass, flattened his nose. What was it, maybe sixty-five feet down? If he jumped out of this window now, he would be in the air for almost exactly two seconds and would hit the ground with a force of twelve thousand pounds—six tons. Such figures came effortlessly now, after years of trying to impress trainees with the awesome kinetic energies generated when "soft" human bodies fall or jump from heights of several stories. Hammond grimaced now, remembering a time when he had tried to dramatize the figures for fire fighter candidates. During a rescue-net demonstration on the Academy's black-topped drill yard, one of Hammond's aides, acting on the drillmaster's secret instructions, dropped a ripe watermelon off the five-story-high drill hall so that it would land wide of the waiting Atlas net. Reacting to the *whuump!* and the spray of red fragments, two of the more impressionable candidates had fainted, one suffering a slight concussion.

The door to Hammond's darkened room slowly eased open, and the man in the doorway watched Hammond's silhouette at the window for a few seconds. He decided to have some fun. *"Don't jump!"* he shouted.

For the second time in less than one hour, Hammond made an involuntary lurch. He yanked his face away from the glass but did not make out who it was. "What the hell do you think—" Then he recognized Commissioner Minot Winston Gault III. Gault apologized for having startled Hammond, and then he helped Hammond back onto his bed. Hammond laughed and waved off Gault's apology. Hammond said that, in fact, Gault was the very man he wanted to see.

From time to time as Hammond talked, Gault smiled at the drillmaster's intensity; could this be the same man he was trying to get into a competitive mood just twenty-four hours ago?

"All right, Rob," Gault broke in. "All *right*. The way circumstances are now, I can back you this far—and no farther. If a thing has to do with *determining the cause of the fire,* okay. That's just completing the part of the job you're already responsible for. Anybody wants to go to war over that, I'll take it. You just make goddamn sure you don't get caught outside that area."

Hammond asked for a telephone, and Gault nodded.

Gault decided not to tell Hammond of his suspicions about Benedetto and the cave-in. Not just yet.

9

PORTRAIT OF SHERI SUE

WEDNESDAY morning came out hot and clear—one of those times Chicagoans can't see the air they breathe.

Dennis Rosewater rattled the nine-foot-high doors at the LaSalle Street entrance. He laid his badge against the glass for the guard to see. The guard pointed to his wristwatch and held up seven fingers: seven minutes till opening. Rosewater shook his head and pointed to the lock. The guard made a helpless gesture. People were just not eager to do Rosewater's bidding; his small size, his mild appearance, and his politeness were very often taken for signs of weakness. However, Dennis Rosewater was not a weak person. He motioned for the guard to put his ear close to the crack between the two doors, and when the guard complied, Rosewater told him in a very quiet, very polite voice that, if the guard did not go and get somebody with some authority, he would personally kick his ass all over LaSalle Street. And so it was that Sergeant Rosewater was the first nonemployee to walk into the hallowed Century Bank and Trust on Wednesday morning.

Once inside the bank, Rosewater told a functionary what he wanted and was ushered straight up to the seventeenth floor, to the reception area of the Trust Department. There, a formidable matron took over.

She seated Rosewater in a private office that was three times the size it needed to be to serve every function but one: to impress. Rosewater was left to wait in isolation, and he wondered if they were trying to impress him or if they were showing their disdain for an undersize young policeman. He had no way of knowing that the trust officer he was waiting to see was on the telephone, answering questions put to him by Chief Robert V. Hammond.

She leaned forward until her breasts touched the glass. The glass felt like it had been chilled, and she said "ooo" very softly, and her nipples stiffened. She leaned over farther until her breasts hid most of the glass, and then she pushed the button that said PRINT. The sound of the fan came up to a controlled roar, and she could hear parts moving inside the device. A page slid out into a tray. She picked up the page and looked at it critically. It was just as she had hoped: The copy quality was superb, and there was no doubt about what you were looking at. She giggled, like a child. Too bad the stationery's not bigger, she thought; so much of me was left off.

As he strode past the giant Picasso sculpture, Detective Sergeant Vernon Hooker glanced up and wondered absently, for the fiftieth time, if Chicagoans were sort of acting out their own version of *The Emperor's New Clothes*. Then he hurried on across Daley Plaza, mumbling. One sweet batch of jobs Benedetto had handed him. In the next few hours, Hooker would ask the

Bomb Squad and the CFD for data on possibly related fires; he would check reports of other crimes and incidents in the subject neighborhood on Monday night; he would have a run made of names he had compiled so far, for criminal records; and he would get the names of police officers assigned to directing traffic during the fire and those assigned to patrol the areas nearby before and during the fire. After which there would be more, much more; Vernon Hooker would shovel a lot of paper before he found out that he had already interviewed the arsonist.

"Busy day, busy day," he chanted softly to himself as he bounced along. "No time to catch a crook."

Robert Hammond wasn't hurrying off to anywhere, but he was at work nonetheless, trying to reason it out.

First, this was almost surely the work of a professional torch. A lot of owners who burn their own buildings do stupid things like setting an obvious arson fire inside and then walking out and locking up neatly behind themselves. And a lot of fires go out before they do much damage. Setting up a good incendiary fire usually takes time and fuel, and both are dangerous as hell to the arsonist. You pour gasoline out on the floor, the fumes start spreading. Just one gallon of gasoline can have the same explosive force as several sticks of dynamite. Some amateurish arsonists learn that the hard way and get kept after school forever. Not this one. In this case somebody broke in or had enough sense to make it *look* like he had, opened fire doors and propped them open, disabled the sprinkler system, used a lot of gasoline in several well-chosen spots in the building, set the fires without causing an explosion, and got safely away. A lot of things to know how to do. This was no spur-of-the-moment thing like breaking a streetlight or punching up an old-timer for kicks; no Molotov cocktail tossed in the window by an employee who got fired; no hastily devised fire to mask a theft here or to cover some other crime nearby; no mattress fire to help some pyromaniac get off. No, this had the tracks of a pro.

The most likely motive was profit. Fire insurance perhaps, but there were other possibilities. Like breaking a lease, getting rid of competition, getting a tax write-off, creating a basis for invoking an "act of God" clause, enforcing extortion demands—a *lot* of possibilities. Still, insurance fraud was probably the best bet.

Hammond telephoned a friend in the insurance industry and called in a favor. Within twenty minutes, Hammond had essential facts on the fire insurance coverage. Insurer: Prairie Fire and Casualty Company. Amount of coverage: two million dollars. Coverage based on independent appraisal report. Insured: Century Bank and Trust Company, as trustee. Mortgagee clause: none.

The call to Century Bank and Trust Company didn't help much.

Next, Hammond put in a call to Arthur "Golden Hands" Moorehouse and gave the man careful instructions.

Hammond waved a persistent fly away again and again. It could be worse, he thought whimsically. If I were at home, I'd be up to my bugles in spiders. And wasps. He shook his head slowly, a salute to the improbability of life in this city.

———————

"I'd heard about secret numbered bank accounts in Switzerland and places but not *here*," said Dennis Rosewater. "Not in *this* country."

Rosewater was fighting to keep the lid on his frustration. This smoothie, this J. Philip Bettersman, knew things that Rosewater wanted to know—hell, *had* to know—but so far Bettersman would cough up not one goddamned thing beyond the nature of the bank's involvement. Century Bank and Trust Company had agreed to take title to the Clybourn Street property as trustee for the owner, to manage it for the owner, and to pass income along to the owner. For this, the bank was paid a fee; actually, the bank simply took its slice out of the rent it collected. And the bank had agreed to keep the owner's name a secret.

Rosewater said, "Well, obviously *somebody* in the bank has to know who the owner is."

Bettersman said, "That somebody is *I*. Anybody else in the bank who has anything to do with the trust knows it, as I said, only as a number."

"Does the bank have many of these numbered trust accounts?" said Rosewater.

"Some," said the trust officer vaguely.

"Tell me please, does the bank handle other properties for whoever owns the Clybourn Street parcel?" asked Rosewater.

"We cannot ethically respond to such questions," Bettersman replied. Then he looked up and away, at nothing, and began speaking in a pietistic tone. "*Trust*. It's the name of our business: Century Bank and *Trust* Company; *Trust* Department. It's also the very nature of our business: *Trust* us with your money; *trust* us with your property; *trust* us to keep our word. Why, it would be as unthinkable for us to violate a confidence as to, as to—*steal*."

Give this guy enough time, he could make you *puke*, thought Rosewater. Sidestepping the specious declamation, Rosewater assured the trust officer that he was not questioning the trust department's mission in general nor was he questioning people's right to privacy. But what about when that right to privacy bangs heads with an obvious public need, Rosewater challenged. "What do you do if you agree to keep a secret like this and—mind you I'm sayin' *if*—you find out you may be a straw man for a racketeer or an arsonist?"

The trust officer conceded that it was an interesting philosophical question but that, as a practical matter, the bank had little choice but to look not only to its ethical constraints but also to its *legal* constraints. "Hell, we could be sued right out of our jockstraps," was the way Bettersman summed it up.

Rosewater asked him if he had ever been legally ordered to reveal such information.

For the first time, the trust officer looked directly at Rosewater's eyes for several seconds. Then he said, in a flat voice, "You seem to me to be a very decent young man, so I'll tell you this much. You'd be wasting your time. I can assure you it wouldn't do you any good."

Rosewater felt that the man was trying to tell him more than the words actually said. If so, he didn't understand it.

GET YOUR FACTS STRAIGHT
(Use Your Library)

Eldert smiled at the sign. Exactly what he was here to do.

It would take some digging. You couldn't just saunter over to the subject index and find what Eldert was looking for; there were no cards between *Incas* and *incest* that said *incendiary*; and there were no cards between *Bolivia* and *bonds* that said *bombs*. And a professional arsonist could hardly afford to ask the librarian: Hey, whatcha got on incendiary devices?

But Eldert Maddox knew his way around libraries. After the incident in which his hands were mutilated, he had faced up to a need for more knowledge; he came to a library for the first time, rather as a virgin to a deflowering, and was no less changed by the encounter: Eldert Maddox fell in love with libraries. He had no doubt that libraries were as close to heaven as you could get in Chicago. They were peaceful, always; usually uncrowded; relatively clean; and free. You didn't have to be rich or famous to get in; you didn't need a reservation; you didn't need to dress up. People always spoke very softly to each other in libraries. They rarely acted as if they were under a lot of pressure. Librarians were mostly polite and helpful. Some were remarkably so; if you asked them to help ferret out something, they acted as if you were involved with them in some holy quest.

Eldert assumed the staffers must sometimes wonder why he was wearing gloves indoors, especially in summer. He had concocted a story about an allergy but so far had had no need to use it. Librarians were probably used to getting some pretty wiggy people, and they were either too polite or too uninterested to ask him about the gloves.

Whenever he could, Eldert had hurried to his beloved libraries and searched and read. Training manuals that the Chicago Fire Department used. Manuals for arson investigators. Military manuals. At first, he read only paragraphs and chapters that had to do with methods of setting fires. Ultimately, he read everything that had to do with fires—setting fires, fighting fires, investigating fires. When he hadn't understood some technical point, he had dug into technical encyclopedias and journals.

Eldert had also found it no problem at all to order books and studies on arson directly from publishers. For this, he had used an assumed name, money orders, and a post office box; but he had grown uneasy about this procedure: Was it possible that it might occur to somebody to check up on who ordered all this stuff?

Sitting in his truck last night, Eldert had remembered something he had read two or three years ago. A couple of the books on arson investigation had made brief references to a device, just giving a name, saying that it was incredibly destructive, and stating that it had been used in Europe in World War II. The possibilities of such a device had so excited Eldert at the time that he had gone after it step by step; first the general encyclopedias, then scientific and technical encyclopedias, and finally manuals on industrial applications that required intense heat.

Eldert remembered that the idea was really pretty damned simple. You just stuffed a case with a mixture of two metallic powders. This was a mixture you could buy right off the shelf in certain stores. Then you lit any part of this mixture, and all of it would burn like a sonofabitch. If a material is going to burn well, it needs oxygen. Well, when this stuff burned, it made its *own* oxygen. And it produced a molten metal that was incredibly hot—two or three times as hot as molten iron usually is, plenty hot enough to ignite any combustible material it contacts, *easily*. There was a really beautiful option too: If you put this stuff in a case made out of a certain metal, it was even more fun because the resultant fire was harder'n all hell to put out. If you sprayed water on it, the burning case would break the water up, break it into chemicals, and actually use part of the water as fuel. As *fuel*.

Eldert needed to go back over the details. He couldn't recall the technical name of the device. He'd look that up first in a textbook. Then finding details in manuals would be easy. Eldert ran a gloved finger slowly down a row of books, looking for his favorite book on arson. It had been written by some local guy. Hartley? Hanson? No, here it is: Hammond.

Peace.
Security.
Warmth.

Hammond's pre-op shot was taking effect nicely. He floated on his bed, and he did not have a care in the world, not a damned one.

10

ORNAMENTS

ON the wall, there were 114 glass eyes and hundreds of fangs, yellow and gray. Dennis Rosewater looked around the room and wondered why anybody would decide it was a good idea to decorate a restaurant—a place where you come to *eat,* for chrissakes—with assorted animal heads and fish heads. With their mouths *open* yet. However, he didn't put the question to Benedetto, who had chosen this place as the spot for Rosewater and Hooker to meet him.

At two o'clock on Wednesday afternoon, the lunch crowd was thinning out as people drifted back to Loop offices and stores. There were seats open at the counter, but the three policemen waited for a booth. They had things to talk over, and it isn't easy to have a private conversation sitting at a counter, three in a row. Besides, whoever spaced those counter seats didn't have a man like Dominic Benedetto in mind.

They were seated by a hostess who looked as if she alone must put one hell of a dent in the profits. Nothing had pulled on her big breasts in recent decades except gravity, but she was not ready to call it quits; her makeup and her dress grabbed for attention. She handed them menus and weighed anchor for the return trip to the front of the restaurant.

Hooker elbowed Rosewater, who sat beside him, and said, "Oughta find yourself a nice girl like that, Rosie, settle down."

Benedetto grinned across at them. "Come on, Hooks, quit pimpin' for yer kid sister and let's get to work."

At Benedetto's direction, Rosewater led off. He reported that the Clybourn Street property was held by the bank in a secret numbered trust and that the bank flatly refused to reveal the name of the effective owner.

Benedetto said, "I'm due at the state's attorney's at three o'clock to talk about another problem. I'll ask him can we do somethin' to twist the bank's tail."

Hooker had laid his menu aside and taken off his glasses. He was giving Rosewater his undivided attention. *"Which* bank?" Hooker asked.

"Century," Rosewater said.

Hooker brought a hand to his chin to help him focus his concentration. Absently, he said, "Huh!"

"Huh, *what*?" Benedetto urged.

"Probably nothing," Hooker said. "But that list I got this morning? You know, suspicious fires in the area lately? Well, when I was looking over the list of owners, I just mentally crossed off the banks as suspects; I mean, *banks* aren't gonna be out setting—"

"Lemme see," said Benedetto.

Hooker pulled pages out of his inside breast pocket, unfolded them to verify what they were, and handed them across the table to Benedetto. Benedetto scanned the summary, then ran a thick finger down the column headed "Reported Name of Owner." The list included names of three banks as trustees, but none of the three was the Century Bank and Trust Company. Next, Benedetto went back and read the few facts set out for each of the three bank-held properties. First, there was an ancient two-story, twelve-unit apartment building.

• 72 •

Heavy damage. Two deaths, nine injuries. Insurance claim paid. Obvious arson, with signs of accelerant poured into both stairwells. Jesus!

Then there was an old five-story industrial building. Completely destroyed. Cause undetermined. No occupants. Insurance claim paid.

A third case also involved an old industrial building, a two-story warehouse, which was completely destroyed. Accelerants detected; probable arson. No occupants. Insurance claim paid.

Benedetto raised his eyes to the two men facing him and started to speak, but the waitress arrived to take their orders, and the conversation was immediately tabled. Rosewater was careful not to order anything represented on the walls. As soon as the waitress walked away, Benedetto said, "This thing is shapin' and we're gonna keep yankin' on it till we see what we got. But I'm gettin' a funny feelin', like maybe we're gonna pull up somethin' that won't fit in the boat."

"Don't worry, Dom," said Rosewater, eyeing the walls with exaggerated distaste. "We can always stuff it and hang it in here."

Benedetto's laugh rumbled up from a subterranean cave. Then the man put his right arm on the table and leaned forward as far as his bandaged side would allow. The other two men leaned in close to listen.

Benedetto said, "Okay, so far we got one dead cop, killed by a fireman on his way to our fire. We got arson. We got an owner who hides behind a secret trust account. Maybe an innocent reason, maybe not. I find out this mornin' we got a sackful of insurance, two million bucks' worth. We got an insurance company won't cooperate with us—"

"Whaaattt?" said Rosewater. "Why in the name of— They ought to be doing cartwheels. We're trying to—"

Benedetto held up a hand and patted the air in front of Rosewater: Calm down. Benedetto understood Rosewater's response all too well; the bald fact was that Benedetto had come perilously close to erupting this morning when they told him that he would have to bring them a subpoena to get copies of the policy, endorsements, memoranda, and appraisal report. He saw it differently as soon as he heard their reason: It is not clear how much information a private insurance company can *voluntarily* make available for a criminal investigation without exposing itself to the risk of a lawsuit. He explained this to Rosewater and Hooker and added that it was not a problem: He expected to be able to get a subpoena from State's Attorney Kleinschmidt, run it over, and get the insurance papers they wanted.

He would also mention the Century Bank and Trust problem to Kleinschmidt. Benedetto handed the summary of recent fires back to Hooker and told the two men to visit all three banks on that list this afternoon. "Don't phone 'em. If we got an arrangement at one of these other banks like at Century, we stand a helluva lot better chance of a guy openin' up if yer there face to face. Hold their hands."

Benedetto slipped up out of the booth and picked up his check. "Okay?"

"What about your lunch?" said Hooker.

Benedetto said, "Gotta see Kleinschmidt at three, and I just thought of somethin' I gotta do first. Besides, Rosie's right. What kinda guy wants to eat his lunch right under a buncha animal heads?"

What Benedetto remembered was that he wanted to telephone the hospital to check on Hammond's condition.

The Flagpole checked her wristwatch. "Actually, you're not supposed to smoke for almost an hour yet."

Hammond's voice was froggy. "I would commit a major crime for a cigarette."

"How about a minor indiscretion?" she suggested archly.

"Who brought that TV in here?"

"Your beautiful but short fiancée."

"The cigarette," Hammond urged.

"Don't tell anybody, okay?"

"Oh, Christ, thanks," he said and added, "I don't have one."

"One fiancée?"

"Not even one."

"Funny, that's not the impression *I* got."

Got from talking to Sheri Sue, Hammond was willing to bet.

Before Eldert left the sanctuary of his beloved library, he looked up addresses of several firms that retailed welding supplies. He chose one in the old South Town section and drove there, parking his *BUSY* truck on a side street three blocks away. He stood across the street from the establishment and watched patrons come and go for nearly an hour. Mostly work clothes. A few shirts and ties—foremen and purchasing agents? Then a character who looked like he had been sent out by Central Casting. Perfect, thought Eldert; I wouldn't have considered such an obvious getup.

A single sheet of paper, folded once. The edges were held together by a huge red sticker in the shape of a heart. It lay on the pillow on Hammond's bed when he was rolled back from surgery but he did not open it till the Flagpole had gone.

He inserted a finger between the edges of the page and broke the heart-shaped seal. He opened the page and—oh, my *God*! Sheri Sue has, she's photocopied her—there was puerile handwriting at the bottom, in pink ink. "All yours," it said, "for life."

Eldert drove to a store on Cermak Road that specialized in workmen's clothing and safety paraphernalia. He bought a billed cap, safety goggles, and a black shop apron. The shop apron had an odor like new tires. It wrapped around his sides and hung below his knees.

On the way home, he stopped at a hardware store and bought a small can of grease.

11

HELPING HANDS

WITH days to fill between tours of duty—usually twenty-four hours on and forty-eight off—and with an appetite for more income, many firemen became part-time tradesmen. One such was Art Moorehouse, a beefy, florid man who smiled easily and talked loudly. Moorehouse had been a fireman for eighteen years now and had worked with a plumbing contractor for fourteen of those years. There were three side effects from his plumbing work. One was a pair of rust-stained hands, from which came the second—his nickname: Golden Hands. The third was that Golden Hands Moorehouse had become the department's *de facto* expert on plumbing and practical hydraulics. Some freak drained the plumbing fixtures so he could ignite the sewer gas? Call Golden Hands. Was paraffin introduced into the sprinkler system to plug the works? Get Moorehouse. Golden Hands's "Three Laws of Plumbing" were considered classic in the fire service: (1) The boss is a sonofabitch. (2) Water don't run uphill. (3) You don't put your hands in your mouth. Back when Hammond had worked as an arson investigator, he had on several occasions called Moorehouse in to help him. In one particularly spectacular case, the sprinkler pipes had been drained of water, then refilled with gasoline.

Moorehouse had answered Hammond's call this morning as if completely unaware that almost six years had elapsed since they last talked. Moorehouse was grinning now as he came shambling into Hammond's room, carrying two brown package-store bags, one clenched in each golden hand. The bags hid the bottles from view but did nothing to disguise the nature of the contents.

Moorehouse announced, as if addressing a convention of teamsters: *"Medicine!"*

Hammond sipped the J&B, savoring the slight bitterness. "Pleasingly superior in kind, Golden Hands. You do anything else in good taste today?"

Moorehouse's recapitulation of his day's activities was as blunt and playful as the man. Following Hammond's instructions, he had gotten a sign printed and erected at the fire scene which solicited information from witnesses and promised anonymity. ("We rigged a light on it, on accounta I figger maybe we hit our best customers at night.") He had gotten Hammond a work-up on recent "funny fires" in the area and Hammond immediately noticed the same thing Benedetto had—that three of the burned buildings on the list were held by three different banks as trustees. And he had contacted a newspaper reporter who had interviewed Hammond about notable fires in the past. The reporter was of Chinese ancestry; and, although the reporter spoke with no trace of accent, Golden Hands reported the gist of the contact in a singsong voice: "He say he honored do interview, be here ten tomolly, flishy-flash. Chief, I ever tellya? I hadda Chinese girl once, and an hour later I was horny again."

From the outside, there were no obvious signs of intelligent life within. It appeared to be simply a long-vacant little two-story projection fastened to the back of a massive warehouse that fronted on Elston—rather like a wart on an old bag. The four walls of the projection had not a single window; one of the four walls was laid against the back wall of the warehouse; the two side walls were uninterrupted brick walls; in the fourth wall was a metal-clad garage door, and beside that, three concrete steps which led up to a bricked-up doorway. The steps were coated with detritus of hard-times nights: green and brown glass, unfurled prophylactics, dried vomit, short butts.

But once in a while there were small signs of what this really was. Sometimes smoke rose out of a chimney that stood several feet out from the warehouse building. And when snow fell very heavily over this two-story projection, it caught light coming up from something behind the parapet walls that hid the roof.

Tool marks on the metal-clad garage door told of unsuccessful attempts to penetrate. Had the would-be intruders been successful in peeling the garage door, they would have been surprised. Behind this one and only door, which could be opened and closed with a remote unit, were a clean garage space, a workshop, furnace, water heater, and a carpeted stairway leading up to the second floor. And upstairs were a bath and two oddly furnished but comfortable rooms with large skylights.

There are scores of such projections and lofts near the Loop that are used as clandestine homes. Want to walk to work, escape yard work, avoid high rents, *hide* from somebody? Often, the residential usage—and some elaborate interior improvements—are kept secret by letting the outside go to hell, dirtying the windows, and piling trash at the entrance. A favorite trick is to urinate in the entranceway until the place smells like a *pissoir.*

None was more secret than *this* place, now the domicile of Eldert Maddox.

For a time, Sid Ruck had used this lair solely as a place where it was safe for his bookkeeper to wrap her big cruel mouth around his joint twice a week. Then, ten years ago, Ruck first met a strange, friendless boy named Eldert Maddox when the boy applied for a job as a night driver for Ruck's *BUSY* fleet but wouldn't answer some of the questions on the application form. Ruck had seen in the young Eldert a night driver of a quite different sort: the cat's-paw in a business scheme Ruck had been shaping. Ruck had moved Eldert into this secret dwelling, advanced him money to live on, told him not to associate in any way with *BUSY* employees or to discuss his work with anyone, and eventually gave him a *BUSY* truck because it was a near-ideal cover for going into any neighborhood at any hour. In those early days, Ruck had come here often, to indicate to Eldert that he cared about him and to give the young man a devious view of Chicago life that would suit Eldert's new line of work. The Chicago of bribing the fire inspector. The Chicago of public employees lopping off trees in the parkway so they wouldn't hide the billboards. Mostly the Chicago of Richard J. Daley. Dick Daley, who could hand millions of dollars of insurance on public buildings to his own son and then tell people that if they didn't like it, they could kiss his ass. Boss Daley, who could park that ass squarely on the black man's face and still get the black man to vote for him in election after election. God, what a *man*, Ruck had said over and over to Eldert. Daley had been the one hero of

Ruck's life, just as Ruck was to become the one hero of Eldert's life. It had not been too difficult for Ruck to turn the twisted, solitary young man into a twisted, solitary disciple.

In their last face-to-face talk, which had taken place here the day before Ruck left Chicago, the fat man mentioned to Eldert that he had a "bought and paid for" city employee. "Who?" Eldert had asked with sudden interest, but the fat man had told him only, "Nobody you'd know, my boy." Afterward, Eldert wondered why Ruck had told him about this at all. It was quite unlike Ruck to divulge anything of a sensitive nature until Eldert needed to know it; Eldert was sure Ruck had had some conscious reason. Was it to impress Eldert with Ruck's power and influence, to keep Eldert subservient? If so, it wasn't necessary. The young man had already given his allegiance, fully.

From the beginning of their relationship, Eldert had worked only for Ruck, which was safer for both of them. No middleman to tip the insurance company in exchange for a reward. No amateurish building owner to make childish mistakes like moving favorite possessions out just before the fire. And Eldert always did his work alone, just as he was doing tonight.

In the secrecy of his lair, Eldert cut the bill off the new cap he had bought and threw the bill away. Then he scrubbed what was left of the cap with soap and water and steel wool. After fifteen minutes of this, Eldert was satisfied that the cap looked used, and he set to work abusing the rubber apron with sandpaper. Then he opened the can of grease.

12

SILVER BALLS

ALTHOUGH the City-County Building would not open to the public until eight forty-five on Thursday morning, certain Cook County employees began to arrive before five-thirty, brought in in police cruisers with headlights poking in the dark. Soon, three teams of county employees were in the hunt—one team on the first floor, another up on six, the third on ten. When things clicked, data moved between the teams sequentially— six to one to ten—like a ball in a triple play. A name on six became a code number on one and a microfilm on ten. Each success brought forth a copy of a deed. All of the deeds involved parcels in a particular North Side neighborhood, deeds which had been transferred to trust departments of banks.

As the pile of photocopies grew, Sergeant Dennis Rosewater's hopes for a quick breakthrough got sick and died. The names of the former titleholders were different on every deed, every goddamned one.

"An *epidemic?*"

"Yes, sir."

"What the hell, exactly, are you talking about?" said the big-bellied man.

The other man, the one in Chicago, explained: "Suppose the rest of the litter got sick and died—all of 'em, all in the same night. And suppose a lot of other dogs that live in the same neighborhood, they got sick and died too. Say the chances of the medics saving 'em would be just about zero. Say they find out somebody poisoned 'em. So what? They'd have to figure it was some nut, just somebody hated dogs or their owners, wouldn't they? Otherwise, why *all* of 'em in the area?"

"This idea, you think it's a serious possibility, huh?"

"Yes, sir, it *is*."

"Hunh. I don't know. Let me think about it, and you call me back tomorrow. Meantime, you go ahead and work on that possibility."

"Yes, sir."

"Pssst!"

As he strode down the tenth-floor corridor, Benedetto heard a hissing noise. He glanced toward the source and recognized Vernon Hooker waving at him from a doorway near the far end of the corridor, on the City side.

"Sound like a poison snake," Benedetto mumbled as he got close enough for Hooker to hear him. "Whatcha doin' *here*? You were s'posed to meet me down the hall, in the records room."

Hooker was eager to tell him the reason for the change: "Rosie's hiding from a clerk in there, had some real romantic plans for him. Looks like a armadillo, but hell, you can tell right off she's a *lady* armadillo."

Benedetto grinned and said, "Rosie, how we ever gonna find you a girl if yer gonna be so goddamn *fussy*?"

Rosewater sat at a small conference table, with papers arrayed before him on the table. Rosewater smiled just enough to acknowledge the needling and said, "I came down here because it *was* a quiet place to work."

Benedetto sat down opposite Rosewater and began pulling papers out of his sling and piling them on the table. He had found his sling a convenient place to carry things, and now he carried an assortment of insurance papers that he had just picked up in exchange for a subpoena. The mound he was unloading on the table grew into an impressive pile.

Standing well out of Benedetto's reach, Hooker said, "You must have a very messy doctor."

Ignoring Hooker, Benedetto asked Rosewater what they had. Rosewater told him: seventeen deeds, three on those warehouses they already knew about, and fourteen more. No two sellers the same.

Benedetto said, "Well, if bein' a good detective was easy, everybody'd be doin' it. How many copies you get?"

"Just one of each deed," Rosewater told him.

"We need three," Benedetto announced. "In a hurry. Who'd you meet who'll give 'em to us fast?"

With a wide grin, Hooker put his hand on Rosewater's shoulder and said, "There's this girl just down the hall—"

Rosewater glared up at Hooker, then scooped up the deeds in an unordered mass and thrust them at Hooker. Hooker and Benedetto roared. Rosewater managed a grin and relaxed. The mild-looking little policeman said, "Dom, while *he* is getting the copies, there's something I'd like to show you."

On lined paper, Rosewater had worked up a summary to help him discover any points of similarity among the deeds. In military columns seventeen lines deep were street addresses, names of former owners, the name of each banking institution that now held each of the seventeen properties in trust, the date of each deed, names of the notaries public who attested to the sellers' signatures, the name of the attorney or other person—if one was cited—who had prepared each deed, the addresses cited in the deeds to which the original deeds should be mailed after they were recorded, and the addresses to which future real-estate tax bills should be mailed.

Benedetto paid particular attention to the list of former titleholders. No two alike, just as Rosewater had told him, nor even similar. Unless some of the names were phony, there was no apparent relationship between the former owners of any two properties. "Okay," Benedetto said, "what've you learned by this?"

"Something that's fascinating," said Rosewater. "In the list of who prepared the deeds—yeah, there—the name of the same attorney comes up four times."

"Who?"

"Name's Emerson Lipford."

"That doesn't ring any bells."

"Not for me either. But listen, it gets better. The address for where to send the original deed after it's recorded? Well, that's the same for *eight* of the deeds. And guess what?"

"The address of Emerson Lipfer?"

"Lip-*ford*. His law office, on Randolph."

"What about *our* warehouse, on Clybourn, the fire that started all this?"

"One of the eight. And you remember those two old warehouses in the same area, on Hooker's list of recent suspicious fires?" Rosewater pursed his lips and nodded sharply twice. Then he continued: "*So,* here we've got seventeen deeds from seventeen different sellers; apparently no relationship. And eight of the seventeen involve the same attorney. Dom, there must be—

what?—five, ten thousand lawyers in Chicago. No way this can be coincidence. It's *got* to mean something." Rosewater was animated, *up*.

"I agree with you, Rosie, but is there some logical reason yer overlookin'? Like, maybe Lipfer—Lip-*ford*—is the lawyer for one or two of the trust departments."

"Oh, boy, I didn't think of that. Let's see—no, wait. Remember, Dom, the Clybourn warehouse and the other two that burned, they're three of the eight that Lipford was somehow involved with, and we already know that they're held by three different banks. Here's a fourth, a *fifth*—"

"Okay, that's not it. Anyhow, point is we need to find out what it does mean. Uh, Rosie—"

"Yes, sir?"

"Good work this mornin'. I've seen worse detectives at your age." Then, for the benefit of Hooker, who had just returned carrying a wad of copies in each hand, Benedetto added, "Hell, I've seen worse detectives *a lot older*."

With grotesque fingers, Eldert dabbed at a patch of grease on his face. *Hell* of a disguise, he thought as he studied his image in the mirror. Why, my own mother . . .

Eldert broke off the thought. He couldn't think of his mother without feeling pain. She hadn't liked him as a child. How would she feel about him now that he was an adult—with funny hands? The *bitch!*

The disguise served two purposes. First, he looked like a shopworker in a factory or a foundry. That would help to avoid suspicion when he stopped at several stores to buy the materials he needed. Second, the disguise made it almost impossible for anyone to see enough of Eldert to decribe him in detail later. The now-grubby cap hid his hairline and most of his hair. The grimy goggles on his forehead and the streaks of grease on his face were a little theatrical perhaps, but they were effective in altering his appearance. Work clothes, the shop apron, and safety shoes hid most of the rest of his body.

And, of course, he would wear gloves.

While Hooker collated copies of deeds into three identical stacks, Benedetto ordered him and Rosewater to make the rounds of all the trustees named in the deeds. "You know what questions to ask. Be charmin', get somebody to talk."

Rosewater asked Benedetto if he had talked with State's Attorney Kleinschmidt about leaning on the banks.

"Yeah," Benedetto said, "but he's reluctant to go that route." Benedetto ticked off reasons the state's attorney had given him. Kleinschmidt saw some legal problems. Also, political pressure or legal action could be damned unpopular with people who are not without influence. Then too, even a court order might not get them what they wanted; the trustee of a secret numbered account may not even *know* the name of the effective owner. Sometimes ownership is buried under another layer, even several layers, and you have to peel it *all* away if you want to find out who the owner is. Like, for example, maybe Bettersman over there at Century Bank only reports to a lawyer, who reports to the trustee of another secret trust in another state, who reports to a lawyer in a third state, who reports to the real owner.

That sort of thing. Maybe that was what Bettersman was hinting at in this case. And finally, Kleinschmidt had pointed out to Benedetto that there are other ways to get at the ownership, ways that hadn't been explored. "Of course, he's right about that last part," Benedetto concluded.

Hooker finished collating the copies. Benedetto scooped up one set of the deeds and pushed them inside his sling. Then he began picking up the insurance papers he had removed earlier and putting them back inside the sling. Watching Benedetto stock his sling with the piles of paper, Hooker grinned archly and said, "Gosh, Lieutenant, you get an attack of diarrhea, you're gonna be all set."

Benedetto rose from the table, and Hooker vacated the room with surprising speed.

———————

Eldert had been very nervous about his first stop. In telephone calls, he had learned that the distributor did indeed stock several parts—tubes, pipes, and other shapes—made out of the particular kind of lightweight metal Eldert wanted in the casings for his incendiary devices. The stuff was used in making optical equipment, luggage, several other products. Eldert assumed that none of the parts was *designed* as a case for an incendiary bomb, but he had hoped to be able to look at various parts to find something he could adapt to his use.

The cover story he worked out seemed to him very thin, but it was the best he could devise. He was an artist, he was making some colossal sculptures, and he was looking for some metal parts that would provide an interesting contrast to the more common metals he was using. He wasn't exactly sure about the shape or shapes he wanted, but he'd know it if he saw it. Could he just look at whatever stock items they had available—say, anything hollow and up to about this long? Eldert had hoped that whoever waited on him wouldn't know any more about sculpture than he did and wouldn't be much interested in it.

As it turned out, the stock part which Eldert found was different from what he had envisioned—smaller and round rather than oblong—but it was almost perfect; it might just as well have been designed as the case for an incendiary grenade. He bought every one in stock: one hundred and eight of them.

The salesman hadn't expected such a sizable cash sale, and he took a sudden interest in this customer who wore goggles on his forehead and who looked like he hadn't washed his face this week. He told Eldert—that was after the money had changed hands—that he surely didn't know anything about making "them art sculptures" but that he assumed Eldert knew that you couldn't use a welding torch on this metal 'cause it could go off like fireworks. Eldert thanked him and was able, only with some difficulty, to decline the salesman's repeated offers to help lug out the several cartons of parts. The truck was parked a block away, and Eldert did not want him to see it.

The rest of the shopping—buying packages of the metallic powder and the ignition materials—had been a snap. Eldert had decided to go only to the larger dealers in this type of industrial supplies, reasoning that they would have more customers and be less curious about an unfamiliar face. And he had tried to choose hours when they would be under some pressure to hurry with each customer.

It was all so easy. So far.

One look at that little kisser would tell you the kid was up to *some*thing. Like most eight-year-olds, he was not good at looking innocent when he *tried* to. What he was doing was sneaking his foot under a rope. A little farther. Just a little farther. And he put his foot right on *the spot.* He risked a look up at Pacucci and was jolted to see the fireman staring directly at him; he was caught. Then Pacucci made a slight smile and winked. In an instant, a dozen more feet slid under the rope to touch the very spot where the Great Chicago Fire had started.

Hell, who could blame the kids? Or adults either, for that matter? Pacucci had seen plenty of adults do the same thing. They believed, as Pacucci did, that this was the exact spot where the most famous fire in American history had begun.

Actually, it was a con.

Oh, there was no doubt—no doubt at all—that the fire that had gone on to eat the Loop and half the North Side had started in Mrs. Catherine O'Leary's little dairy barn on this site, here where Chicago's Fire Academy now stood. However, no one was all that sure at which *one spot* the infant fire had first begun to feed. Should we draw the "x" right here? Or maybe over here? Why draw an "x" at all? Well, for one thing, there is more dramatic punch in pointing to one spot—here, this spot right here—than to say that the Great Chicago Fire started around here *some*where.

And so an "x" was drawn. Or, to be exact, a cross was drawn: the emblem of fire services everywhere, that cross with curved edges which is called the pattée-nowy. The cross was painted in a convenient spot on terrazzo flooring, in the main hallway of the ground floor of the Fire Academy. And this cross is guarded by a yellow plastic rope hung on stanchions made of the nozzles of fire hoses. And thousands of children and adults come each year to this spot. And the pattée-nowy is being worn away by their feet—the little feet and the big feet—slid under the yellow plastic rope.

The guide for visitors was Federico Pacucci—"Fireman Fred" to the children. Fireman Fred had the credentials for this assignment: icebox chest, good hair, proud posture, and a love for the fire service that knew no qualifications, no contingencies. He had a primitive acceptance of tradition and authority; in seven years of guiding visitors to the yellow plastic rope, it had not once occurred to Fireman Fred to wonder if the Great Chicago Fire could have gotten its start over there by the library or down here by the drinking fountain.

As Pacucci fielded questions, his love affair with the fire service made the air around the children almost glitter. "See, the Great Chicago Fire, it happened a long time ago." Pacucci drew out the word "long" for the children. He rejoiced in the safety of familiar questions and practiced answers. "Back in 1871, over a hundred years ago. They had wooden houses and wooden sidewalks and funny-looking fire engines pulled by horses. It's different today, darling. Whatever happens, the Fire Department can handle it."

Fireman Fred was sure.

But then Fireman Fred was also sure that the pattée-nowy marked the exact spot where the Great Chicago Fire had started.

13

PUZZLES

AT seven-fifteen on Thursday evening, Sergeants Vernon Hooker and Dennis Rosewater sat on barstools and compared notes. Rosewater had started out with the copies of seventeen deeds. One of the deeds was the one transferring the Clybourn Street warehouse to the Century Bank and Trust. Rosewater had taken the other sixteen deeds around to the seven banks named in them and learned that eight of those deeds were to secret numbered trust accounts—the same eight deeds that bore one lawyer's name and address. This group of eight included both of the old warehouses burned in recent fires of questionable origin. Rosewater now felt absolutely certain that there was a pattern here that did not result from chance. He had learned no more from the trust officers he questioned today than he had learned from Bettersman at the Century Bank and Trust yesterday; each had told him only that the real estate in question was an old industrial building being managed under the terms of a confidential trust. Every effort Rosewater had mounted to learn more from the trustees, every gambit he tried, had crashed, it seemed to Rosewater, with all the ignominy and finality of elephant "pies" hitting concrete floors at Lincoln Park Zoo.

Of the eight transfers Rosewater had pinpointed as germane, Vernon Hooker had contacted seven of the sellers. All seven had sold through brokers—five different brokers. Not one of the seven sellers knew who the buyer actually was. And neither did the brokers. Not a single one. Each of the seven agreements had been made in substantially the same way. The property was offered for sale for a time and shown to various prospects. Maybe another broker called up the listing broker and arranged to show the real estate to a prospect, either with or without the listing broker present. However, none of these showings had resulted in an acceptable offer, at least not *directly*. Then, as if from heaven or hell, the listing broker was contacted by an attorney—"guess *who*," Hooker said—who made an offer on behalf of an anonymous client. Naturally, the broker and seller were curious—mostly, they wondered if somebody was buying up properties to assemble a tract for some big project—but they had decided to accept the offer; and at the closing, the property was deeded to a trustee.

In the *eighth* case, Hooker had been unable to make a seller contact because that seller had died over two years ago. "Dom'll never accept that excuse," Hooker moaned.

Half of Chicagoans with phones aren't listed in the directory, by their own choice. But Hammond found both numbers.

He dialed Gault's home number and was told by a woman that Gault was out. Hammond asked her to leave a note that he had called and would call the commissioner at his office in the morning. He hung up and wondered if the woman who answered the call was Gault's wife. He realized that he didn't know anything about Gault's personal life, not even his marital status. And he didn't really know much more about the man's professional life, beyond the fact that Gault was a lawyer, was very well connected, and obviously enjoyed a luxurious life-style. Gault was the first fire commissioner in modern times who hadn't come up through the ranks. Hammond had mixed feelings about that.

Next, he called Golden Hands Moorehouse at home and told him to begin checking out sales of burned warehouses. "I want you to contact every broker who had anything to do with the sales to those trust departments that own buildings that were torched, find out who they showed those buildings to—*everybody* they showed them to, including other brokers. I figure there's a good chance our mystery buyer wanted to see inside those buildings before he bought them. Did he look at them as a prospect or maybe get somebody else to act like a prospect and look at them *for* him? What we want to know is, can we make some person as looking at all three of the bank-owned buildings, or some of them? Or did our mystery person even *talk* with the brokers?"

Golden Hands said, "Chief, you really think a broker's gonna remember everybody he's showed through a building, let alone who he *talked* to?"

"Answer is, I don't expect a hundred percent. But we've got two things going for us. Some brokers keep track of prospects pretty methodically, write it down when they just *talk* with a prospect. Sometimes a prospect will try to get around the broker's commission by waiting till the listing expires and then going to the seller. Sometimes a broker'll show a prospect something and then, for one reason or another, that prospect will try to buy it through *another* broker. Also, somebody who's only kind of interested now may be a good prospect later on if the price gets reduced or something. Or say a guy's only mildly interested in *this* property, he may be a great prospect for some other property in the future. And some brokers like to be able to show a seller that they showed a property "x" number of times and talked to "x" number of prospects—show they're really hustling, keep a seller in the boat. So some brokers keep very careful records. Another thing that could help, these brokers must have spent some time wondering who was making those offers. Maybe they've got some ideas. And Golden Hands—"

"Yes, sir?"

"Tread lightly, please. We're possibly overstepping our authority just a bit here."

Possibly, *hell*, Hammond thought.

So far, his efforts had produced exactly zip. Well, that was hardly unusual in an arson investigation, he knew. You can plod through the fog for days, *months*, and then, all of a sudden—*ta-daa!* Question was, was that Neanderthal, Benedetto, going to beat him to the ta-daa?

14

BAD FRIDAY

Friday Morning, July 17

Fire-Setter Probably "10-48"
KILLER FIRE WAS ARSON
The spectacular fire that Monday night claimed a
block-long Clybourn Street warehouse and figured
in the death of a policeman was the work of an
arsonist. So says Fire Chief Robert V. Hammond,
Chicago's nationally recognized authority on arson, holder of two of this city's highest decorations
for valor, and author of . . .

Sheri Sue stopped reading and began to count up
how many copies of the newspaper she should buy on
her way to the hospital this morning.

. . . in an interview in Chief Hammond's hospital
room. Hammond suffered ankle and head injuries
when part of the burned-out structure collapsed
on him while he investigated the fire scene in the
early hours of Tuesday morning.

Golden Hands was relieved that the article did not
reveal *which* hospital.

Hammond said the cause of the fire was "unques-
tionably incendiary," and he made a plea for additional information of any nature whatsoever on
circumstances surrounding Monday night's fire.

Dominic Benedetto snapped his paper and snorted. The silly sonofabitch doesn't even know when he's out of the game.

Meanwhile, in the air-cooled quiet of his limousine, Minot Winston Gault III compressed his lips and nodded. Hammond had done reasonably well in not appearing to be overstepping. Any criticism coming from this he could handle. Gault guessed that Hammond had given the reporter the psychological-profile stuff in a calculated effort to make the arsonist or arsonists look as unthreatening as possible to potential witnesses.

> Hammond said arsonists are often physical cowards. "Arson is a sneaky crime," he pointed out, "in which the perpetrator doesn't have to face his victims." He said studies have shown that many arsonists have physical deformities. Hammond believes that even most professional torches are probably at least "slightly 10-48" (10-48 is an old radio code used by police and fire services to refer to demented persons). According to Hammond, "fire-for-hire" arsonists . . .

Eldert Maddox's mind was a zoo of catalogued injustices and fears, and this unlocked the cages. After ten years of reporting on his fires, newspapers had become a sweet source of excitement and strokes for him, and he was unprepared for anything like this. He shook his head violently in denial. He trembled, and he wept, and he raged in tortuous paranoid ramblings about one injustice, then a seemingly unrelated one, and yet another. At the end, he sought to deal with the things that had hurt him most by swearing revenge on them. Burn down the reporter's house was what he *ought* to do. Or the newspaper building. No. Oh, no; what he *would* do was get Robert Hammond.

———

Maybe the timing of Sheri Sue's visit really didn't matter. Maybe it would just have happened the same god-awful way another time. Maybe. But the timing sure didn't help.

Hammond struggled around his hospital room trying to get the hang of crutches. And as if one such activity summoned another, he began struggling with memories of another time in another hospital. Oddly, what came back to him most vividly now were a man's eyes. Hammond had gone in for tissue-matching tests in preparation for donating a kidney for transplant into Suzanne's little body. The physician in charge of the program was telling him, in esoteric terms, that tissue from his wife or another donor might be more compatible than his, and Hammond had caught a change in the man's eyes. When you're an arson investigator, which is what Hammond was then, you get so you watch the eyes; the pupils enlarge and the blink rate speeds up when people lie or when they get stimulated. Unable to shake a feeling, he had pumped his own physician for details, then gone to work on a chemist in the police lab. "Biologically impossible," pronounced the chemist; a man with Hammond's blood type could not have a biological daughter with Suzanne's blood type.

Arguably, Hammond had gone crazy for a time.

But it was a kind of crazy that society tends to accept, sometimes even to exalt, as selflessness. The crazy of martyrs and saints. He could love people in the abstract—"mankind"—but he could no longer love or trust a person.

Can you love an innocent child with a whole heart, then just quit? Hammond was ashamed of it, but, at least in his case, the answer apparently was yes. Nevertheless, as part of a divorce settlement, Hammond volunteered to provide so richly for Suzanne that his lawyer, unable to dissuade him, finally insisted on making a record of his objection, fearful that others would someday look back on the matter and wonder what in the hell had been wrong with Hammond's counsel.

Through a church group, Hammond "adopted" foster children by mail—first one, then three more. The children wrote letters. He didn't answer them.

He had to keep people out in front of him, far enough away. And he accepted a soul-rotting, compacted loneliness as willingly as another man might present his arm for a vaccination, and for roughly the same reason: Hammond sensed that aloneness was the price he had to pay to reduce the chance of enormous hurt.

Four and a half months after he had seen the last of his wife and "daughter," a follow-up investigation had brought Hammond to the victim of an arson fire a few months before, a six-year-old Chicano girl. Whose eyes were locked wide open, as if the nurses were still picking her scabs. Whose debridement operations had left her with a face of melted putty. Whose belts of grafted-on skin were contracting, drawing that face down, inexorably, toward her groin.

A lot of burn-unit nurses can't take it for more than a few months, and some parents can't either. The mother and father had gone somewhere. Hammond, on the edge of bankruptcy, borrowed six months' wages and gave the money, anonymously, to provide for continuing plastic surgery. He hadn't debated it; it was simply something he had had to do. What he *had* wrestled with was whether he could continue seeing the child, could give her more than the money. He couldn't, and he tried—tried hard—not to think about what that meant.

There had been times of intense interest in objects—a Vasarely or a Gold Coast condominium or an Eames chair could not threaten to do more then give pleasure and would be the same tomorrow, next year—but that fix never lasted long.

What worked for Hammond was work. Something he *could* do. Hundred-hour weeks powered by a desperate zeal. Student, then teacher, eventually the CFD's unofficial saint-in-residence. And because Hammond was bright and attractive and by the circumstance of several senior officers growing old at about the same time, Hammond's dedication carried him rapidly up, up from his nadir to the third-highest spot in the CFD. Like a Polaris missile shot off the bottom of a foul septic pond. And now after what?—seven, eight years, he could still catch a whiff of where he'd been.

The thoughts followed him as he paddled out of his hospital room.

By the time he reached a small lounge, he was grateful for a chance to rest. He was sitting there thinking what a debacle his pass at family life had been when Sheri Sue found him a few minutes before noon. She rushed up with sweet smells of summer, from her perfume and that of a sheaf of roses that had cost her several hours' pay.

By some perversity of Nature, Sheri Sue had decided that now was as good a time as any to make her speech, to tell him she thought it was time for their relationship to, well, *evolve* was the word she had chosen. She had been psyching herself up for this meeting all morning, and she was stretched dreadfully tight. She had to get the speech going right now or she'd never be able to. Here goes.

"Patient Information," the voice cooed. "May I help you?"

"Can you tell me, please, the room number for Robert Hammond?" The man's voice was polite.

"Just a moment, sir. Uh, I'm sorry, sir, but Mr. Hammond's listed as not having visitors at the present time."

"Oh. Well, I just wanted to send some flowers or something. You have his room number?"

"Well, we would be glad to be sure he gets them."

Her mentioning the word "marriage"—that was a slip.

His citing "our agreement" and implying that she was breaking the rules—that was pointless, really.

And her telling him he would be miserable without her—now, that sounded like an ultimatum.

But his asking for his key back—well, that was lunacy.

She stood up and spilled the roses, tried to pick them up but kept spilling some of them because she was crying so hard. As Hammond struggled to get up on his crutches, she gave one of the crutches a vicious kick and Hammond pitched forward and cracked his head on the tiles. And she thrashed at him with the roses and raved about his being so smart about books and stuff but dumb as a box of rocks about other things. She stopped swinging the broken plants and stood hunched over him, sobbing. A black behemoth in a candy-striped uniform hugged Sheri Sue and drew her through the ring of curious patients and staff, crooning to her that everything was going to be all right. Two staffers tried to help Hammond up, but he waved them away.

How about a nice basket of fruit? Better yet, a *book*; a book'd be such an appropriate gift for that maggot.

Question was, what kind of a *mechanism* to use. A

time-delay device wouldn't be worth a doodley-squat. You couldn't be sure the bomb would be close enough to Hammond when it was set to go off; it could be parked on somebody's desk waiting to be delivered to Hammond's room, or it could explode in Hammond's room while he was in the can or who knows where.

An antidisturbance device wouldn't get it either. For that, Hammond would have to be the first one to move the object. You couldn't be sure of that even if you took the thing into the hospital, right into his room, and set it up. Damned hospitals are *ant*hills.

How about a booby-trapped package? Hammond opens it and catches a shaped charge up his nose. *If* Hammond opens it. Too many helpful people around. Besides, you send a package to a guy with Hammond's savvy, guy who's written all about terrorist devices, you have to figure there's a chance he'll feel hinky about opening it. Another thing: With the low explosives Eldert had ready access to, the amount of charge you could build into the average gift-size package might not get the job done. And Eldert Maddox wanted to do this job right. Let that fuckin' slanty-eyed reporter do a column on how they were picking up pieces of Robert Hammond all over three, four zip codes.

———

Damn it! He would have to pass their station to get to his room. Maybe they hadn't heard what had happened down the hall. He figured that, if he just put his head down, kept his eyes on the tips of his crutches, and walked slowly by, maybe—

"Well, Casanova returns," announced the Flagpole.

"Lock up your women and girls," called out the Shrub.

Hammond stopped walking and dropped his head lower to signal his resignation.

Then the Flagpole's manner changed abruptly; she helped him to his bed, attended to the head bandage, which was working loose, then caressed his face with a cold swab that made the scratches burn. While she made a deft check on his vital signs, she told him with good humor that she hoped he would stay closer because he was easily their most popular guest. He'd had three disappointed visitors within the last hour alone: Dr. Shorter, who had smiled, said he'd check on Chief Hammond tonight, and said he hoped the patient would be back by *then*; Mr. Gault, who had chuckled; and that fireman with yellow hands, who had laughed out loud.

She didn't know about a fourth visitor, who had decided there was too much going on now and left without talking to anybody.

15

BLOODSUCKERS

"EIGHT hundred thousand bucks?!" bellowed Benedetto.

A secretary seated fully twenty-five feet away jumped and then pressed a palm flat on her bosom to still her heart. One just didn't expect sharp noises in the quiet luxury of D. Dexter Denning's offices; certainly it was not common to yell out dollar amounts at the top of one's voice. Dominic Benedetto hadn't meant to raise his voice, not at all; it had just sort of burst out of him.

On the desk between Benedetto and Denning lay a copy of the three-hundred-and-fifty-seven-page appraisal report—which said the burned-out Clybourn Street warehouse had been worth two million, four hundred thirty thousand dollars—and a copy of the two-million-dollar insurance policy. D. Dexter Denning was a golfing and bridge crony of Police Commissioner Edwin Keller, who had arranged this appointment for Benedetto because Denning was one of Chicago's most knowledgeable industrial brokers and appraisers.

Benedetto changed his voice to an animated whisper and said, "You're tellin' me it was actually worth only eight hundred thousand bucks?"

Denning, as unruffled and impressive as his offices, said, "That's about what it would have gone for in a typical sale."

Benedetto leaned forward and laid his right hand on the duplicate of the appraisal report. "Then how the hell do you account for *this*?" he whispered.

"I don't *have* to."

"I don't understand," said Benedetto. "Are you suggestin' the people who did this appraisal're *crooked*?"

"That's not the point."

"Then *what*? Come on, D's, *talk* to me."

Denning told him that there was nothing all that unusual here, not really; most appraisals for insurance purposes aren't based on what a property would *sell* for; you figure up what it would cost to replace it with a *brand-new* building, and you subtract something for age and condition and for certain items that insurance policies usually don't cover.

Denning explained that insurance appraisers often make any deductions from the brand-new cost in a mechanical way that doesn't recognize a bad design, a punk location, weakness in demand, or other economic factors which can make a building worth a hell of a lot less than a brand-new cost. "Hell, Dom, insurance appraisals of three, four, five times what a building would sell for—they're not that uncommon on old buildings."

"Well, yeah, but—" Benedetto began, then fell silent.

Denning smiled at Benedetto—he was beginning to like this outsized policeman—and waited patiently for Benedetto to work out his point.

And Benedetto did. "Isn't there another side to this? S'pose *I* owned this buildin' on Clybourn, okay? It burns down, wasn't my fault. Now, I gotta go out and buy some other buildin', *don't* I?"

"Yes," Denning agreed. "But do you have to buy a *brand-new* building? Or an existing building that's a lot more desirable than yours was? Christ, Dom, I can show you dozens of old buildings like this you could buy for around eight hundred thousand dollars. If you want to replace your lost building with a far better one, *fine*. Put some money with the insurance proceeds and *get* one. But anytime you can get two million dollars for a building by burning it or eight hundred thousand by selling it—and you're going to have some expenses and delays if you *sell* it—well—" Denning held his hands out, palms up: *You* tell *me*.

Benedetto nodded, then went back at it on a different tack: "Look, I buy a buildin' for eight hundred thousand, okay? I wanna insure it, but I don't wanna pay for a lotta extra insurance, do I? Well, the insurance appraiser says two million, four thirty, and I say, 'Screw that!' I know if my buildin' burns down, I can buy another just as good for eight hundred thousand. So, unless I'm a goddamn crook, I buy only eight hundred thousand worth of insurance, right?"

"Well, you *could*," conceded Denning. "But the insurance companies do their best to make that alternative unappealing. They may give you a lower rate per hundred dollars of insurance if you insure up to some percentage—80 or 90 percent—of the 'insurable value.' If you don't go for *that*—if you're so stubborn you insure your building for eight hundred thousand dollars because that's all it's *worth*—then you'll get it in the ass if there's a partial loss. Let's say an honest-to-God accidental fire burns off three hundred thousand dollars' worth of your building. Then the insurance company says to you, 'Oh my, isn't that too bad! We're just so goddamn sorry, but you only insured for one third of the *insurable value*, so we're only obligated to pay you one third of the loss.' So they pay you only one hundred thousand, and you go whistle for the other two hundred thousand. Sounds like a fairy tale, doesn't it? But that's about the way it works. And the moral is: If you want to be covered against partial losses, you have to insure your building for a lot more than it's worth."

"That's no moral," Benedetto snapped. "That's an *im*moral. You figure these insurance appraisers, they know about this?"

"Oh, hell, yes," said Denning.

"And the insurance companies?"

"Sure."

"Why'n the fuck—?"

"That's the way it's been done since who knows. Everybody's making a living, so why try to change the system? Don't glare at *me*, Dom. I'm telling you what I think *they* think. So far, the insurance companies just raise the rates to cover the arson. The more insurance an agent writes, the more money he makes, right? So the higher the appraisal, the better he likes it."

"Simple as that, huh?" said Benedetto.

"Not really," said Denning. "But you see the problem. Fact is, somebody who really understands these things can do a pretty good job of predicting which buildings will get burned on purpose."

Dominic Benedetto sat quietly for a time then, his face going through changes. At last he spoke quietly and sadly, "Insurance company in this case, they pocket premiums on two million bucks of insurance on a building worth less'n half that, right? And if I'm successful in this investigation, the company may not even hafta pay off on *that*. Fuckin' *bloodsuckers*!"

Denning looked thoughtful for a few moments, then nodded. "Yes," he agreed, "bloodsuckers."

FOR LEASE

Vernon Hooker frowned at the sign and smacked his palms on the steering wheel. This was the eighth and final old chromo on his list, and he knew his idea was a dud. Most of the other buildings were occupied, at least, but if there was anything linking the tenants to the person they were looking for, he sure as hell couldn't see it. The first one he had looked at, a big pile near Elston and Webster, had been deeded to the trustee just two years ago, but it had been occupied by the same tenant for thirteen, fourteen years. That tenant had told Hooker, with a grin, that his rent was far below what the building would rent for now because the present lease had been signed almost ten years ago. The tenancies in three of the other buildings were essentially similar to this. Two of the buildings were vacant. The rest had short-term leases and month-to-month tenancies arranged by the trustees. No two buildings were rented to the same firm or individual, and no relationships among the various tenants were apparent.

One of these days, Hooker told himself. One of these days I'm gonna come up with something that'll pop Benedetto's eyes, make 'im really *proud* of me.

16

HOME ALONE?

"You don't seem to be getting much *rest* around here," said Dr. Shorter with a devilish grin.

Hammond could imagine the kind of gleeful briefing Shorter had gotten from the Flagpole and the Shrub.

Shorter continued: "I'm going to let you go home tomorrow morning, even though that's going to be unpopular."

"Unpopular?" said Hammond.

"I told one of the nurses," Dr. Shorter explained. "She complained that whenever I get an eligible young guy in here, I'm in too big a hurry to get him out again.

"However, Rob, I want to see you next week—my nurse will work out an appointment before you leave the hospital—and I want you to limit your activity. Stay home. Use your crutches every day in several fifteen- or twenty-minute sessions. No acrobatics." The devilish grin again. "Try to relax and enjoy the time. If you have any problems with the head or the ankle, don't be a hero; call me. Okay?"

"Okay."

"I'm going to give you a prescription for pain. You *will* have somebody staying with you, or coming in regularly to look after you, won't you, Rob?"

"Sure," Hammond lied.

Sheri Sue was a little surprised not to find—and be found *by*—the Trash Truck hall patrol on a Friday night. Did the old bag actually take time off? Outside Hammond's door, Sheri Sue bent down and set her burdens on the carpet: a brown paper bag of groceries and cut flowers wrapped in green tissue. Rob had to eat, and he loved flowers; he would appreciate her making the place nice for him when he eventually came home.

She dug in her purse for a key, the key that Hammond had asked her for this morning. If he ev-v-er made that mistake again, she would, by God, stick this key right in his *eye*. She was the best possible person for Robert V. Hammond, she told herself with supreme conviction, and he had better, by God, start acting like it.

Two matters were pressing on her mind as she worked the key in Hammond's front door: She was afraid of those spiders—desperately—and she had to pee—desperately. She tiptoed inside without the bundles, snapped on a light, and crept warily over to the patio doors, ready to turn and flee at first sighting. No spiders, at least none she could see. Sheri Sue caught a deep breath and let it slide out. As she relaxed she was immediately aware of her other problem. She pressed her knees together, held her left hand against her crotch, and walked back to the front door in tiny steps, like a child imitating a geisha. She brought the bundles just inside and locked the door. Then she did her geisha walk down the hallway to Hammond's bathroom. As she took the handle to open the bathroom door, she felt pressure on the knob—as if someone had hold of the knob on the other side. She released the knob, took a step backward, and asked in a strained voice, "Is— someone there?"

Minutes before midnight, Golden Hands telephoned a report to the drillmaster. "No luck so far, Chief. Talked to about a zillion real-estate people and nothing. Couple remember showing your buildings to some circus-size fat guy, but they couldn't come up with a name. Only reason they remember him at all is he was so fat he had trouble getting through some places. Chief, you hear the one about this ex-*tremely* fat Arab? Well, he goes into this whorehouse—"

But Hammond didn't even hear the rest. His eyes were opened wide, looking at nothing. He was thinking about "some circus-size fat guy."

A MAN'S HOME

ELDERT Maddox put his hand over the *B* and then slid it over the *USY*. The yellow *BUSY* lettering was raised slightly from the blue background paint. He'd have to do something about that, sooner or later.

Eldert put his hands in his trouser pockets and began pacing around the *BUSY* van, which stood in his covert garage. *Thinking* pacing. On this Saturday morning, there were only two crucial decisions remaining for him. One was whether to repaint the van. This time out, the truck would carry his load of silver-colored balls, and he needed to get from place to place swiftly; there was no way he could do the job without having the truck with him all the way. Trouble was, that big *BUSY* lettering might stick in witnesses' minds. He *could* sand off the lettering and put a fast coat or two of paint over the whole body. But that would only substitute one risk for another; on balance, it would probably *increase* the risk. What Eldert most needed to do was to get his job done and get away without being stopped and without being identified personally. So what if somebody should remember afterward that there was a *BUSY* van in the neighborhood around the time the fires broke out? There were a lot of *BUSY* trucks. Unless somebody took down the license number on his vehicle, they had nothing. And even the license number would lead them nowhere; it was in the name of a company that lived in a Post Office box and had one asset: this vehicle. Left as it now was, the *BUSY* truck provided maximal cover; it looked like a vehicle that might be called to any neighborhood at any hour. If there was no demonstrable need for it to be there, one could say it was there because of a prank call or because the driver had misunderstood a radio transmission. On the other hand, a van painted off in some solid color and idling outside a closed business establishment at night fairly screamed at the police to have a look. Eldert decided to leave his *BUSY* truck the way it was. However, he *would* buy a large aerosol spray can of blue paint tomorrow— something as close as possible to the color of his truck. Then, after he'd done his job and was driving out of the city, he could turn off at some secluded place and spray paint over the *BUSY* lettering. That'd have to do until he could give this baby a proper paint job.

The other important decision Eldert had to make was when to strike. He had little left to do, and he felt that waiting around would not help his nerves. He decided. To Eldert, making the decision was almost a palpable act, like lighting a fuse. A timer began clicking in Eldert's mind; a countdown had begun.

Sunday night, he decided. *Tomorrow night.*

———————

Hammond lolled in the back of the heavy air-conditioned auto and smoked. Gault had volunteered his driver to see Hammond safely home from the hospital, and Hammond had accepted gratefully. Hammond figured this second ride in Gault's car had to turn out better than the one Monday night. Just four and a half days ago? That wasn't possible.

The windows were tinted, but the morning sun dazzled. Hammond closed his eyes and let his mind go.

When the auto bumped up into the short circular drive in front of his condominium, Hammond opened his eyes and noticed more than a dozen people standing in the shade of the entry canopy. Portable TV cameras, still cameras, and recorders hanging in shoulder slings—*press*. The appearance of an arriving vehicle galvanized the reporters, and they charged it like Mau Maus—only to be jerked back as if by invisible chains. They began to move away from the auto crablike, looking warily at Dominic Benedetto as he bore down on them. Even with windows closed to hold in chilled air, Hammond could make out that Benedetto was speaking sharply, telling the reporters something to the effect that he would talk to them later but that in the meantime they were not to—Hammond missed part of it because the driver was asking him if he would prefer to leave. Hammond looked from the drive to the building entrance; then noticed cars and vans, unmarked but obviously city-owned, parked along the drive; turned back toward Benedetto and the press people—to find Benedetto's massive face just outside the window looking in at him. Benedetto nodded—a serious, almost formal gesture—and opened the door a few inches. Unwelcome July heat scrambled around Benedetto to dive in.

"What *is* it?" Hammond's tone was not polite.

The policeman showed no hostility. "Let's talk inside, Chief." Then he added gently, "Please," and Hammond knew that something had changed.

Hammond declined offers of help from both Benedetto and the driver, got out, and poled his way to the glass-enclosed lobby. The reporters did not approach him, but he could hear their cameras working and could hear voices speaking softly. The door was swung wide by a sometimes-doorman whom Hammond barely knew as someone named Jerry. As Hammond and Benedetto came into the welcoming cold of the lobby, Hammond spotted two men sitting in a far corner: George, the night doorman, and some strong-looking guy he didn't know. Hammond stopped in the middle of the lobby and faced Benedetto.

Benedetto spoke quietly, deferentially. "Chief, I need to talk with you a few minutes."

In that moment when Hammond weighed his urge to tell Benedetto to go fuck himself against his curiosity and concern, Benedetto held out a paw toward a black vinyl-covered bench along a wall, and he said the magic word again, said it very nicely: "Please."

Curiosity and concern won. "You want to come upstairs?"

"No," Benedetto said quickly. Then, more carefully: "Here would be better for a minute."

They sat, and Benedetto began with a gentleness that puzzled and worried Hammond, and he filled Hammond in as briefly as he could, guessing that getting through the essential facts as quickly as possible might be a kindness to Hammond. A woman had been found dead on the sixth floor. The night doorman had been brought over and had identified her as Hammond's blond girl friend. She had apparently been struck in the face, then strangled. Evidently sometime last night. Her body was found in the sixth-floor trash room, had apparently been moved there. From Hammond's apartment. There were tool marks on the lock on Hammond's front door.

Benedetto decided not to go any further for a few minutes. He put his good hand on Hammond's back, not so much to console him as to protect him in case he lost consciousness. It was almost an axiom in this sort of situation that the guys who seemed the toughest were the first ones to hit your shoes. And Hammond looked awful.

The other policeman, the one sitting across the lobby with the night doorman, saw that Benedetto had stopped talking and got to his feet. Benedetto shook his head just once, and the man sat down.

———————

If Eldert was going to practice-drive the area in daylight—to choose the best route, then to drill on that route until he felt easy with it, and finally to time the run—it might be safer not to use his *BUSY* truck. Eldert had had no experience at stealing vehicles and getting rid of them. How about renting a car or truck for just this purpose? Not ideal but probably less risky than using the *BUSY* truck or skipping the rehearsal runs. He telephoned a truck rental location in Evanston and reserved a panel truck for Sunday.

———————

A uniformed policeman stood guard at the elevator. When did he come in? Hammond wondered. Riding up in the elevator, Benedetto introduced the homicide officer, but Hammond didn't get his name, and there was no exchange of greetings. The man told Hammond he was sorry and sounded as if he meant it. Hammond gave him Sheri Sue's full name, told him where she lived and worked. Another uniformed policeman was standing guard outside the elevator on the sixth floor. Lab men were working the corridor. One of them took Hammond's keys from him and unlocked his unit. The homicide officer told Hammond he'd like Hammond to look at his place with them and tell them if anything looked different—"You know, odd or out of place or missing." Hammond pointed out the bag of groceries and the package of flowers on the floor as items that somebody had brought in since Monday. He worked his way down the wall and touched the cut flowers, then squashed a handful of blooms in his fist. Benedetto read Hammond's gesture as simply one of acting out pain, and he judged that Hammond's reactions to the news of the girl's death were not faked.

Making a cursory room-by-room inspection, one of the lab men noticed an odor. He sniffed and touched until he found a wet patch of carpet in the hallway, just outside the bath. He dabbed his fingertips in the wetness, brought the fingers up to his nose, grimaced. "You got a *pet*?" he called out. Hammond shook his head. The lab men and the two policemen held a muted conference in the hallway in which they discussed why somebody would piss on Hammond's rug: It could have been the result of the victim losing control of body functions; maybe it was an act of defiance by the killer; it could even have been somebody with a *specific* grudge against Hammond, like the arsonist Hammond had gone after in the newspaper yesterday. One of the lab men said it might be possible to determine sex and blood type if they could get up enough of a sample of the urine. He'd give it a try.

Eldert was a little surprised.

The silver-colored cases were so light when hollow,

but once he had spooned in the metallic powder, the grenade was heavier than he had expected. No problem for a building with windows on the ground floor if there was no webbing or plastic over the windows. Probably no problem for one-story buildings with only clerestory windows or windows in a sawtooth roof. However, you'd play hell trying to lob one of these babies up much higher than that—say, onto the roof of a two-story building or through a third-floor window.

Did he need some kind of a sling or catapult to do that? One things was sure: He wouldn't have time for breaking in through doors or for scaling a ladder. What if you didn't fill some of the grenades full? Suppose you just filled them to good throwing weight and then put in some inert packing. You could put colored markings— say, with paint or fingernail polish—on the lightweight grenades and then use those for the higher shots. Why not?

18

A KIND OF SPORT

"WHY are *you* in on this?" Hammond asked Benedetto.

Benedetto inclined his head to suggest they move away from the others, and he led Hammond into the bathroom, closed the door. He motioned Hammond toward the commode. Instead, the drillmaster hoisted himself up and sat on the vanity counter, then lifted his left leg onto the counter. Hammond did not even respond when Benedetto asked him if he'd like something to drink. Benedetto sat on the commode and mused about what an inelegant picture this made: a one-armed cop and a one-legged fireman getting together in a crapper to talk about murder.

Benedetto said, "As soon as Saler found out a ranking member of the Fire Department was involved, he called Keller, and Keller put out a call for me."

Hammond didn't recognize the name Saler, but he knew who Keller was: Police Commissioner Edwin Keller.

Benedetto got off the commode and switched on the vent fan. Hammond's cigarette had already fouled the air. Besides, Benedetto hoped the fan sound would cover noises the lab man was making as he worked to get urine out of the hall carpet.

Hammond spoke so softly that Benedetto had to ask him to repeat it. "Is she—is the body still here?"

Benedetto shook his head slowly.

"Was she raped?"

Benedetto held up an empty hand and said, "Can't tell for sure yet."

Hammond had some understanding of what that meant. No gross indications of forceable rape: no marks on the body, no gobs of semen or blood on the body or clothing, where you might expect them. Hammond knew the lab men used the same kind of hand-held ultraviolet scanner to look for body fluids that he had sometimes used himself to search for hydrocarbons and hot spots. They would shine that goddamn thing around his apartment looking for traces of blood and semen. Well, they'd sure as hell find 'em. Under ultraviolet light, even *dried* semen stains will glow a nice eerie blue-white. Was that why Benedetto had brought him in here? Were they out there standing around in his bedroom right now—look there! and there! and there!—and snickering and elbowing each other? Would they take Benedetto aside later and, with leering grins, tell him the Chief was a regular Old Faithful?

"You were last here on Monday night?" Benedetto said.

Hammond looked evenly at the policeman. He made no response for several seconds. Then: "Am I a suspect?"

Benedetto's empty right hand came up again. "All possibilities, Chief. As you know."

Benedetto understood from Hammond's manner that he was opposed to any further discussion of the point. Neither man spoke for minutes. There was the fan noise, and once the sound of a telephone ringing three times. Hammond supposed they were answering his phone. He didn't care.

"Why the trash room?" Hammond asked.

Benedetto's reply was interrupted by a soft knock on the bathroom door. Benedetto opened the door far enough to stick his head out. He pulled it back in and said, "Chief, you got a car?"

Hammond nodded. Benedetto told Hammond that, on the chance they were dealing with a whacko who was really out to get Hammond, they were doing a bomb and poison check.

Hammond shifted on his perch, dug out a set of keys. "Down in the garage, second floor. Gray Buick."

Benedetto passed the keys through the doorway, and his great dark paw came back into view holding a scrap of paper. The policeman looked at the slip of paper, and his face caught in a moment of concentration. "Gotta make a call," he mumbled as he yanked the door wide and strode out into the hall. There was the sound of impact, an angry complaint from the lab man working on the urine spot, and Benedetto's voice: "Oh, Jeez, *sorry.* I forgot you were there."

When Benedetto came back into the bathroom minutes later and closed the door, he told Hammond he had just returned a call to his wife. She'd been trying to catch up with him since shortly after he'd left home this morning, he related, because somebody had called her and given her the name of a guy who was supposed to be behind the fires.

"Who?"

"Anonymous. She said it sounded like a man tryin' to change his voice."

"No, who's *behind the fires?*"

Benedetto hesitated a beat, then answered: "The name she got was Ruck, Sid Ruck. It may be nothin'. I called downtown, and they're seein' what they can dredge up for me."

The drillmaster stared past Benedetto and pictured

"a circus-size fat guy" named Sid Ruck. He forced the picture away. Why had it taken hours to relay the message from Benedetto's wife? They apparently had no problem finding Benedetto when they wanted him to get over *here*.

Moments later, Hammond repeated his question: "Why the trash room?"

Benedetto decided to tell him. "Whoever did it tried to put 'er down the incinerator chute, looks like."

Hammond closed his eyes for a moment, then opened them and asked, "Who found her?"

"Woman lives in six-fifteen. Name's Forter."

Hammond was almost positive she was the woman he and Sheri Sue had called Trash Truck. Sheri Sue had often wondered aloud what it would take to get in and out of this place without that woman catching her, Hammond remembered. So Trash Truck had caught her one more time. The final time. It was a silly goddamned point to get to Hammond, he knew; it had no significance. He was losing control. He told Benedetto to get out, let him alone.

———————

Half a million windows watch the lakefront, and they never blink. There are so many things to see; who can have a window on the lakefront and not want a pair of binoculars?

But in the oven heat of midday, so many things were happening along the beach on Saturday afternoon that no one paid attention for long to a man who wore only swimming trunks and gloves and appeared to be practicing for some sport. He was throwing a silver-colored ball high into the air but making no attempt to catch it, just letting it come down in the sand with a ka-whop!

The man tried one-handed hook shots; then two-handed throws that started down between his bent legs, close to the sand; even push-away shots from chest height. For a time, he threw only to feel the weight of the ball and to see how high he could throw it. Later, he moved close to a great old tree with puny foliage and seemed to have chosen a specific part of the upper branches of the tree as a target for each throw.

There was no danger of the object going off until the firing device was attached and activated; it would take a very high temperature applied to just one tiny spot to begin the fireworks.

After almost two hours of this labor, Eldert Maddox sat down in the shade of the tree, resting his bare back against the trunk. He felt the sweat running down his body, and he savored the mild euphoria that physical exertion can sometimes buy. He held up a hand, palm down, in a familiar test of "nerves." Like an iron bar, he decided. For a time after that girl had surprised him at Hammond's last night, he hadn't been sure he'd get his body under control again the rest of his life.

As his fellow Chicagoans strolled past him along the beach, he regarded them with that lonely-exciting sense of detachment that most people feel only as a stranger in an unfamiliar city; after ten years here, Eldert Maddox remained essentially alone, an outsider in his own town.

Eldert remembered reading that once, a long time ago, hordes of Chicagoans had fled onto this very beach to try to escape the Great Fire. Men had even buried their wives and children in the sand with only their faces sticking out and then lugged pails of water from the lake to pour on them.

He noticed that the leaves that hung down near him were limp and gray. This huge tree was dying of thirst while it stood here, helplessly anchored to this spot and looking at what lay spang in front of it: *twenty thousand square miles of water.*

Slowly, Hammond's face slid sideways into the mirror. One red eye. Then the other. Squinting against smoke coming up from the cigarette in his lips. The face looked *bad.*

"Trick or treat," he said.

Hammond had climbed down off the vanity and stood over it, his hands flat on the counter for support, weight on his right leg. He worked the handle on the cold-water tap and let the water run. He wet a fingertip, drew it across his forehead, then wet it again and touched his eyelids. Hammond felt a trace of irritation, as he always did when he noticed how low the basin was. Why do they feel they have to design bathrooms for small children and dwarfs? I'm not that much taller than average, he thought, but if I stand up straight, the bottom of the goddamn basin is down around my goddamn *knees.* But he didn't stand up straight; he let his head hang down, and he focused on the stream of water, wanting it to occupy his mind, wishing he could get in it and ride away from here. A drop of water formed on his nose and fell. Another drop formed in its place. And fell. Hammond lifted his face to the mirror, saw that he was crying. The cigarette was still burning, but it was wet. Shifting his hands on the vanity, Hammond leaned over far enough sideways to drop his cigarette into the commode—sptttt! He tripped the handle of the commode, and his world blew up. The roar of a locomotive going right over Hammond. The front of the commode disappearing and a hole appearing in the wall opposite it. Hammond slamming against a wall. A power saw starting up in his head. Smoke and a bitter odor, not altogether unpleasant to him. Benedetto putting a hand on his face and telling him to lie still, that everything was all right, that the damned thing had apparently missed him completely.

Eldert rose, stretched his back muscles, and spanked the seat of his trunks to knock the sand off. Before he quit throwing the ball, he had fixed in his memory a particular limb, the highest he had been able to throw the ball to with an acceptable degree of accuracy. How high was it? Thirty feet, forty? Closer to thirty. Was it as high as a second-story roof? Or a third-story window? Yes. He knew it wouldn't be too difficult to make an accurate estimate of the height, almost to the inch, but he saw no need for that.

He went back to work, practicing a sport that nobody recognized. People didn't pay much attention to him. Why should they?

19

OH-OH

HAMMOND refused to see a doctor, said what he needed was a *plumber.*

When Benedetto drew him up off the bathroom floor, then started to lift him bodily with just one arm, Hammond objected. However, he did accept support from the policeman as he hobbled to a chair in the living room.

"You got some brandy or something, Chief?"

Hammond inclined a thumb toward a bronze Li-Huan cabinet beside the entry. On the off chance the killer had poisoned some of Hammond's liquor, Benedetto searched for an unopened bottle. Finding none, he shrugged, chose a bottle of cognac, and poured a few ounces. He offered the glass to Hammond, got no response, set it on a table where the drillmaster could reach it. Then Benedetto padded back to the cabinet, held the bottle up to the light, then brought it to his nose and sniffed at it, shrugged again, and took a deep pull on the bottle.

"Uh, you want some company tonight, Chief?"

"No."

Benedetto pointed out that there was at least a slim chance the sonofabitch could come back. Hammond showed interest in that and asked if Benedetto could get him a shotgun.

It took Benedetto a dozen strides to cross Hammond's living room. Looking out the glass doors, he could see nothing beyond the blue-carpeted balcony but blue sky and blue lake.

"Boy, you sure live *high*, Chief."

Momentarily, Hammond wondered if Benedetto meant high in elevation or high in cost, then remembered: Of course Benedetto knew which floor they were on. Hammond did not want this conversation. He made no response.

"Yer family rich or somethin', Chief?"

"I came into some money a while back, invested it wisely."

"An inheritance from a rich uncle, huh?"

"Something like that."

Benedetto hulked around an Eames chair to inspect a still life that looked like somebody had set a dinner table and then somehow squashed it into two dimensions. It was signed by somebody named Braque. Benedetto sighed. The world was so goddamn full of stuff that guys like Hammond understood and guys like him didn't.

Hammond saw the bundles Sheri Sue had brought in, still lying by the door. He wondered if he should put the flowers in water, then thought about Sheri Sue thrashing at him with roses. He swallowed hard and looked up to find Benedetto watching him.

"You got something on your mind, Benedetto?" he challenged.

"Yeah, Chief, I do. Now it's my turn to ask *you*. You wanna help me on this case?"

A few changes of undershorts. Toilet articles. Half a dozen pairs of gloves. Eldert packed only one suitcase.

He bagged and boxed everything else in his clandestine domicile and loaded the truck for a trip to the dump. Into the *BUSY* truck went the accumulation of ten years here: his books; a bale of newspaper articles reporting on his fires; and every device, material, and tool he would not absolutely need to have with him on the run tomorrow night. He wanted this place to be as barren of personal touches as a new motel room, because it was part of one of the buildings to be burned, and there must be nothing left behind to tell investigators about Eldert Maddox. No one must know except himself and one other man. That was enough for Eldert. He could count on the approval of Sid Ruck; on a great deal of money—which wasn't so important in itself because Eldert had money saved, but which was important as a means of keeping score, a measure of *worth*—and on a three-month vacation in St. Louis, where there must be some fine libraries too. Being an arsonist was a lot like being a spy: If people find out you're good at your work, you're not good at your work.

"Guy's white. No record. Fifty-three. Grew up in Chicago, cruddy neighborhood over by Humboldt Park. Last few years here, he lived in Kenilworth, *ver*-y fancy place. Moved to Florida seven years ago—place on the west coast—but he still owns a company here." Dominic Benedetto paused and looked up from the file lying across his thick knees. The other three men—Hammond, Hooker, and Rosewater—sat silently in Hammond's living room and waited for Benedetto to continue.

"I had a policewoman call around, locate an employee who works for that company, say she was in Ruck's high school graduating class and was workin' on this reunion thing, had to get up to date on Siddie. Gal who works at Ruck's company gave her Ruck's Florida address, said he hadn't been back to Chicago for seven, eight years and then asks if Ruck was already real fat when he was in high school. Yeah. Says now the guy's got six chins and a waist just one or two sizes smaller'n the equator."

"What kind of company?" Dennis Rosewater asked.

"One of those board-up outfits," said Benedetto.

Hammond added, "You've probably seen their trucks around fires. They say *BUSY*."

"Oh-oh," said Hooker. He said it softly but in a tone that caused the other three men to stop talking and turn to look at him. Hooker said, "There was a *BUSY* truck there. The night of the fire."

Hammond and Benedetto looked at each other. Then Hammond nodded encouragingly at Hooker and said, "Go on."

So Hooker recalled for them that Chief Hammond had told him to check out people and vehicles in the neighborhood. He had seen this *BUSY* truck driving down Elston and waved it over and talked to the driver. A young man, he remembered. He had an impression the guy was fairly big, but he couldn't be sure, since the man hadn't gotten out of the truck. Nothing very special about him. Said he didn't know anything about our fire, was on call to somewhere else. Hooker hadn't seen any reason to question him further, had let him go.

Benedetto almost asked Hooker the obvious question: Did you get a name or a license number? But he knew the answer: If Hooker had gotten some identification, he would have *said* so. And the way Hooker was sagging in his chair, it was obvious that he felt he had failed them.

"Come on, Hooks," Benedetto rumbled, and he put a catcher's-mitt hand on Hooker's shoulder and agitated it roughly. "Don't be a dumb ass. In the first place, it's understandable you didn't find out who that driver was. And in the second place, you're *gonna* find out. Can you recognize that driver?"

"Yes." There was no uncertainty in Hooker's reply; it was a statement of fact.

"Good," said Benedetto. "Startin' right now, you get to work on *BUSY*. Don't say anythin' about Ruck's connection. Right now, our story is we're reinterviewin' everybody who was in that neighborhood Monday night, Tuesday morning. Ask their cooperation in findin' that driver."

"It shouldn't take long to find him," said Hooker, feeling better. "But that's not all we're interested in, is it?"

Benedetto said, "No. It's as good an excuse as any to talk to people there. Talk to supervisors, secretaries, drivers, everybody."

"Okay, Dom," said Hooker. "Besides the driver, what am I looking for, exactly?"

"Goddamnit!" roared Benedetto. "You're a detective. You tell *me*."

Hooker began slowly but got up speed. "Uh, well, does this guy Ruck come to Chicago? Does somebody from here go down there, to Florida, to see him? Signs of how the company's doing financially. For instance, are they hiring or letting people go? Do they have modern equipment, or are they patching up old stuff? And when I find out who that driver was, I might learn more about him from his coworkers than I do from him."

"See?" said Benedetto, stabbing an enormous index finger painfully into Hooker's chest for emphasis. *"See?"* The finger again. Then Benedetto said with gruff affection, "Hooks, if you'd work at it, you just might become one helluva detective—"

"Right," said Hooker.

"—like *I* have," finished Benedetto. He turned and grinned at Hammond and Rosewater.

"Jesus," muttered Hooker playfully.

"Whaaaaat?" snarled Benedetto, wheeling on Hooker.

"Jesus, I'll never be as good as *you,* Dom," said Hooker; and all four men laughed.

"Mr. Messenger, sir."

"Yeah. How are ya? Look, I haven't decided one hundred percent, but leave it this way: I don't call you tomorrow, you go ahead."

"Yes, *sir.*"

20

SUNDAY DRIVER

EVERY street. Every alley. He weighed alternatives until he believed the route was as good as he could choose. Then he drove it four more times. First the buildings around Elston. Then across the North Branch of the river to hit the buildings in the Clybourn Street area. He made all the stops he would need to make tonight and, at the end of each sweep, he was headed east on North Avenue. The first three times he made the drill run and turned out onto North, Eldert braked and circled back in his rented truck to rehearse again. But not the fourth; this time he kept right on rolling east. He had done his work here, and he would slip down south to the neighborhood where the other buildings were targeted. East through a grab bag of establishments and dwellings to the Gold Coast. Then south along Lake Shore Drive with the cliffs of affluence high on his right, Lake Michigan low on his left. Where Lake Shore Drive takes a whimsical jump to the left, Eldert went straight, onto Michigan Avenue and the Magnificent Mile. Whose fashionable stores take the play away from State Street. Where miniature Italian lights replace the leaves of the trees in winter and great ice shards come racing down the tapered sides of Hancock Center and wallop the sidewalk in spring. Where there still stands a sandstone water tower that refused to pack it in when everything else around it fell down and died in the Great Chicago Fire. Past 900 North Michigan, where Richard Daley's twenty-one-year reign died on the floor of a doctor's office. And on past the offices of a library system with a hundred thousand books missing. To the north edge of the Chicago River, where a black man became the first permanent settler in what was to become the second largest black metropolis in the world. Across the river, which now flows *in* because Chicagoans got sick—both literally and figuratively—of drinking their own excrement and changed the direction the river flowed. On down stately Michigan Avenue, past the Art Institute's two bronze lions, which are not so much in demand now as they once were as symbols of Chicago. Past a park area built on debris of the Great Fire. And on south, with prestige falling away with each block now. So quickly, it's all gone. Michigan Avenue?! Why, this bunch of dirty old buildings could be anywhere. But if you think *this* is seedy, just keep going south and you'll think Chicago lost a war. No, turn left, go one block east to Indiana Avenue, turn again, and *there*, there they are: the rest of the buildings to be burned tonight.

The gears were making noises that worried Eldert. He would be relieved to get this piece of junk back up to Evanston and walk the few blocks back to where he'd left his *BUSY* truck.

As Eldert finished his rehearsal and pulled away from the last of the targeted buildings, he said in his mind: See you tonight.

———————

To get the map ready, Hammond and Benedetto hurriedly added colored markings with felt-tip pens and then stuck the map on a piece of illustration board.

While they were trying to walk it down the street and into City Hall—half-lame Hammond and one-handed Benedetto—the wind nearly took it away from them. But they got it into Room 105 and fastened it up on a wall where it could easily be seen by the only three others who would attend this hastily called meeting: State's Attorney Kleinschmidt, Fire Commissioner Gault, and Police Commissioner Keller.

Gault began the meeting by saying he was agreeably surprised to see Chief Hammond in attendance. "Chief," Gault said, "which of you would like to conduct the briefing?" Hammond responded by telling them they were about to hear the beginning of one of the most fascinating stories in Chicago's history and that they would help write the ending—one way or another. Then he told them that Benedetto would take it from here—Hammond paused and grinned—because Benedetto seemed to need experience. So everyone looked at Benedetto, who had to deal suddenly with a variety of impulses. One was to pull the training aid down off the wall and *feed* it to Hammond. Another was to laugh. What Benedetto *did* do was to get up there in front of that colorful map, grin, and say to them, "Chief was hurt real bad, so let's humor him. Rest of us know it's usually the cop who *does* stuff and the fireman who tells a good story." Kleinschmidt, Gault, and Keller were amused by Benedetto's agility but not half so amused as the drillmaster.

With his characteristic bluntness, Benedetto told them the parts of the story he knew. And then: "There's three things we're most concerned about now. We don't know how big this is, we don't know how much time we got, and we don't know who's doin' the actual burnin' for Ruck. We think Sergeant Vernon Hooker may actually know what the torch—or *one* of the torches—looks like, but we don't have a name yet and we gotta *find* the guy. That's why we're askin' for more help."

Police Commissioner Keller spoke up: "I assume you're talking primarily about *police* help, Dom?"

"Yes, sir," Benedetto answered. He guessed that Keller was probing for some advantage.

Kleinschmidt said, "How many men, Dom?"

"We figure minimum six," said Benedetto. "But we could sure use ten." Gault, Kleinschmidt, and Hammond noted the "we" and assumed it referred to Benedetto and Hammond. They were pleased. Keller was not pleased.

Kleinschmidt said, "Dom, you mean six more than you have now or six *total?*"

Benedetto grinned at him and said, "*Ten* more'n we got now is what we could really use."

Kleinschmidt also grinned and said, "I really didn't mean to try to hold you to the minimum. Ten, huh?"

"Ten *policemen,*" complained Keller. No one looked at him or responded in any other way, and this irritated Keller still more.

"And what would these men do to help you?" asked the state's attorney.

Benedetto answered: "We figger we get men to work full-time on each a' the three problems. We need to keep after records and interviews to find out what other Chicago properties are involved. We need somebody lookin' for our torch. And we need at least six men to start with—two on each shift—to keep an eye on the buildin's we already know about. We wanna talk with Mr. Kleinschmidt about maybe somebody down in Florida keepin' an eye on Ruck, even a tap if possible, about if it's okay for us to take a photo of Ruck around to all the brokers, and about how we can get more outta the bank trustees and the insurance companies and maybe even the insurance appraisers. But right now, right this afternoon, we're talkin' *minimum*."

Fire Commissioner Gault said, "Have you considered the possibility of confronting this Ruck?"

Benedetto looked to Hammond, and this time Hammond fielded the question. "Yes, sir. Obviously, that course would have the virtue of discouraging the burning of his buildings—for a while. It might obviate putting men in to watch them—for a while. I don't know how we'd be sure of that, though."

Gault said, "The mayor wants to see us break some arson cases; that's how we got into this thing in the first place, isn't it?" This was said for the police commissioner's benefit. Then: "There's really no way of knowing how long we'd need to keep a watch on Ruck's buildings, is there?"

"No, sir," said Hammond.

"How soon would you want these men?" asked Gault.

"Immediately," said Hammond.

Police Commissioner Keller was stung. This was moving ahead without his active participation, and they were talking about allocating *cops*. Keller knew he had no choice but to cooperate here, but he wasn't about to be *dictated* to. Keller cleared his throat noisily to get attention, then spoke with the attitude of a largehearted parent announcing to his young children that there was ice cream for dessert: "How about we get you three more men on Wednesday and add another three by Friday?"

Hammond did not show the gratitude Keller expected. "Sir," Hammond said, "I'd feel better if we could get started tonight."

The police commissioner reacted as if he had been slapped in the face. He pushed out of his chair and bellowed at Hammond, "Who the *fuck* do you—"

"Ed-win, Ed-win," Gault crooned. "Have a little pity for this young man. He gets so preoccupied with things like murder and arson that he sometimes forgets his manners. Now, *I've* never had the problem *myself,* but I remember hearing about a young police captain a while back who had it. Seems that he was so vocal about the city needing more police officers he came this close to becoming a civilian. If I remember right, some people even called him Keller the Yeller. 'Course, that was—"

Keller was placated, and a deal was struck: Four additional policemen would report to the task force on Monday, then four more on Tuesday.

Vernon Hooker turned the dusty compact into a parking lot three blocks west of the *BUSY* offices. The crushed stone topping looked new, *sounded* new. He spotted Benedetto's car and parked near it. Hooker got out, crunched over to Benedetto's car, and got in.

"You're late," grumped Benedetto.

"I'm having a *BUSY* day," said Hooker, and he threw up an arm as if to ward off an expected blow.

But Benedetto laughed at Hooker's small joke and asked the balding man if he had done anything useful lately.

In fact, Hooker had much to report. "*BUSY* has sixteen vehicles in all. Twelve are those panel trucks with the big yellow *BUSY* letters on them. Other four are a semi, a dump truck, and two company cars. They're all insured on one policy. I got a list of these sixteen vehicles and checked them against the books— well, against a depreciation schedule. I also checked registrations. Apparently that's all the vehicles they've got."

"You talk to drivers?" asked Benedetto.

"All but two," said Hooker, "which isn't bad considering this *is* Sunday, Dom. None of them are the guy I stopped that night, and all of them say they don't even *know* a guy looks like that, drives for them. I asked are there any part-timers. No. I asked if anybody quit since that fire. No. Any backup trucks? No. So what we got is one of three things. A: somebody borrowed a *BUSY* truck. Naturally, all the drivers deny this; there's a strong company policy against it; you get caught with somebody else driving your truck, you're out on your ass. B: There's a thirteenth truck floating around somewhere. Or C: I'm mistaken about what I saw."

Benedetto said, "Which you think it is, Hooks?"

Hooker looked into Benedetto's eyes and said, "I am not mistaken."

Benedetto nodded and said. "I believe you. That's it for *C*. What about *A* and *B*?"

" I just don't know, Dom. Normally, I'd say the idea of there being a secret truck sounded melodramatic as hell, not the kind of thing to bet on, but this whole thing is melodramatic. I just don't know."

Benedetto worked over several points aloud. "So it could be important, or it could be as harmless as somebody loanin' his *BUSY* truck to a friend for a quick run and not wantin' to admit it. I s'pose we could ask guys in the radio cars to check *BUSY* trucks whenever they see 'em. That'd be a lotta busywork, though. Uh, you get a chance to look at mug books yet?"

"Yeah," said Hooker with no enthusiasm.

21

A NIGHT SO BAD

Clak!

The metallic sound took Sid Ruck's attention. It was the taxi meter switching to a higher fare. Ruck smiled. He liked the symbolism of the taxi meter. Life was a taxi ride. You ride, you pay. The bigger the policy, the higher the premiums. You get "x" number of buildings burned, you *pay* for "x" number. And tonight, the more Ruck drank, the more he would pay. Ruck was on his way to Tampa to celebrate how Rockefeller rich he was about to become.

He had spent the afternoon reviewing appraisal reports and insurance policies, pausing often to savor his own cuteness in planning this detail or that. And he had looked at the payoff photos and wondered if there was a chance that so many fires at once might goose Straight Arrow into some kind of action. Not as long as I've got him by the balls, he had decided. Remembering now, Ruck reached out a cupped hand and, ever so sweetly, he said in his mind, Now, we're not going to hurt each other, are we, Straight Arrow?

Clak! went the meter again and Ruck chuckled quietly, sending rhythmic little tides out to sea on an ocean of flesh.

Four additional policemen were due to report on Monday. In the meantime, Vernon Hooker and Dennis Rosewater were taking shifts at the City Hall-County Building, working with volunteer county employees to sift through public records looking for titles that might be witting or unwitting fronts for Sid Ruck. When Rosewater relieved him at 10:00 P.M., Vernon Hooker left to visit three apartments: a quick no-no with his longtime sweetheart, a beer with his newest girl friend, then home to his wife. The thing that was bothering him: He was late with the rent on all three apartments.

What's going to *stop* it? Not the prairie on the west. And not the lake on the east. A wind on its way to Chicago can get a hell of a good running start.

Every so often, someone will point out that the epithet "Windy City," was hung on Chicago by a New Yorker—this to suggest that, in truth, Chicago is no windier than anyplace else. Just try to tell that to somebody who's seen Lake Michigan when it jumps over the Outer Drive. Try to tell it to a utility-line repairman or an insurance claims adjuster. Try to tell that to somebody who pays the utility bills for a glass-walled apartment up in the sky. And especially, try to tell it to any poor soul in Chicago on a night like *this*.

All Sunday afternoon, pedestrians had had to struggle just to move about. Stores closed early. By 8:30 P.M., fifty-mile-per-hour winds were howling down from the north, and gusts up to twice as heavy snapped off parched limbs and made power lines and TV antennas dance and dance until they couldn't take it anymore. Emergency rooms had a run of eye problems, a workman blown off a roof, a nun whose habit became a kite.

Board-up companies were backed up; they were agreeing only to try to get to calls when they could. O'Hare closed down, and "continuing" passengers were helped to airport hotels. Movie theaters closed after the early show. Restaurants sent the help home. The city was crouching down for a bad night.

The wind had become even more violent by the time Eldert Maddox went out, shortly before eleven, to see if there would be a call from Sid Ruck. Eldert was awed by the weather and had ambivalent feelings when no call came. For almost an hour after struggling home, Eldert weighed the pros and cons of going through with the plan tonight. It would be hard work just to move, let alone throw the silver-colored balls accurately. On the other hand, there would be precious few witnesses out there tonight. The roar of the wind would cover the noise of breaking windows and of crackling flames. Once you got a fire going tonight, it would spread, and it would be harder'n hell to put out. Eldert came to see the wind as an *ally,* to believe that Nature had blessed his plan. With the wind howling its encouragement outside, Eldert final-checked his *BUSY* truck. This would be the night.

The book flew through the air with its pages fluttering, struck the wall with a *whopp,* and fell to the floor like a stunned bird. The gentle Hammond, book lover and book writer, was now a book thrower. He snapped off the light, then lay in the dark and listened to the wind rattle his bedroom windows. For the past two hours he had lain here with pillows under his left ankle and tried to read a new book on fire service administration sent by his publisher. But his mind kept coming back to Sheri

Sue—and it formed, against his will, hideously graphic vignettes of what must have happened to her here. And even in the less painful interludes, thoughts about Sid Ruck would not let him alone.

Hammond listened to sounds of the wind screaming in from the north and throwing body blocks into his building, shooting grit hard against his windows. Fire fighters sometimes refer to the cruelly cold, snow-up-to-here days of winter as "fire weather." But the hazard is of a different order when the wind is blowing *this* hard. And to make matters worse, the city was powdery dry right now, and the ambient temperature was high. The chances for a conflagration are much greater after a long dry spell, as there was before the Chicago Stock Yards Fire; if there is a strong wind, as in the Great Chicago Fire; if the humidity is low, as in the Chicago Grain Elevator Fire.

Something hard hit the side of the building and rattled along it.

His thoughts swung back to guilty ruminations; the way he failed people who had had the misfortune to be intimate with him, he deserved to be alone and despised.

Hammond was finally easing down toward sleep when he remembered the shotgun Benedetto had reluctantly gotten for him. He found his crutches, labored out to where he had left the weapon, checked the safety, and brought it back and laid it on the floor beside his bed.

———————

Almost a quart of Scotch had rolled across the fat man's tongue, and that tongue had become loose. Encouraged by the raucous laughter of his companions,

Sid Ruck was growing progressively louder, progressively more gross.

"Chicago is so fuckin' dirty, they think the flag is red, *gray,* an' blue!" he shouted.

His companions laughed.

"If I owned Chicago and hell," he announced, "I'd sell Chicago and live in hell!"

His companions laughed harder and slapped the table.

"Chicago, *shit!*" the fat man roared. "If the niggers'd quit fuckin' the Mexicans, there wouldn't *be* any Chicago!"

His companions were convulsed. None of them noticed the two black men sitting at a table nearby, two black men who exchanged a look and motioned for the waitress.

Forty minutes later, the fat man rose to leave and wobbled out into the night. He was savagely beaten and died from his injuries two days later, never having learned what happened that night in Chicago.

22

THE RED WIND

THE creature had no chance for a normal childhood. Within an hour of its birth, it was full-grown and stark raving mad.

The spawn of Eldert Maddox, it had a curse: It could not stop eating, or it would die. And the more it ate, the bigger it grew. At first it doubled its size every few minutes. And like any youngster, it loved to run and jump and play. At ten minutes of age, it could run upstairs. At thirty minutes old, it could gather itself and bound from one rooftop to another. At forty-five minutes, it could race a fireman for a block and beat him. At first it crackled with delight; then it *roared*.

It soon turned vicious. Learning to leap and charge in unexpected directions, it could go on by a building and then jump back and take it by surprise. It loved to tear down an alley and grab several houses at once, from the back. Then, even while it was devouring them, it would be looking around for still more victims, desperately hungry. It killed people when it could, which was often; and when it couldn't, it drove them back, outran them, jumped over them.

What drove it mad was the wind. The north wind force-fed it until the youngster stood hundreds of feet tall, then set it rampaging in the direction of the Loop, bent forward and sucking up huge columns of super-heated air as it ran. The fire and the wind became one: the Red Wind. And men had no more chance of putting out the fire than they had of putting out the wind.

The bombing run on the North Side was supposed to have been roughly in the shape of a "U." In rehearsal, Eldert Maddox had worked his way down the west side, along Elston; then crossed the North Branch of the river and worked his way back up, along Clybourn. However, when it came to the real thing, Eldert almost gave it up after he had made only an apostrophe.

Things began going wrong almost at the very top of the "U." The wind made the *BUSY* truck shudder, and it threatened to bowl Eldert over each time he stopped and got out. He had little trouble chucking the balls through ground-floor openings, but any other throws— those at upper-story windows, roofs, skylights, sawtooth windows—proved difficult in the wind. On the third stop along Elston, the wind gave Eldert a hard push as he threw at a second-floor window and spoiled his aim. The silver-colored ball thwacked the block wall just inches to the right of the window and fell back down to the pavement and lit up the night street with a dazzling light of fireworks. Eldert had stood there in the brilliant light, indecisive, helpless and a car had gone past, down Elston, not more than two hundred feet away. If the driver called for cops, Eldert had only minutes to es-cape. He jumped into the *BUSY* truck, drove a block and a half north, and pulled over to think, to decide what to do. Abandon the plan—for tonight? He had stripped his home and set it afire, the first to go. The terrible wind was causing a lot of confusion tonight, and there were few people on the streets. He would give it another try. He drove the *BUSY* truck back to the third building, activated the firing device on another ball, and threw it at the same window. It struck the block wall on the *other* side of the window, and it fell and hit the street with a sharp noise and began to roll. Eldert stood there helplessly, just watching. The thing fizzed brilliant white fire and rolled in a drunken pattern as wind fought with gravity, rolled down the street toward Elston Avenue. Eldert leaped back into his *BUSY* truck and drove the two hundred feet to Elston and made a lurching left turn. Three drivers in southbound lanes were waiting at the intersection for what they assumed was some sort of oversized emergency flare.

Maybe Eldert turned left because that was the way he had rehearsed it. Or maybe it was luck. Certainly, Eldert had no conscious thought of resuming the bombing run when he had bolted. But he did. As he rolled past the side street where his fourth stop was scheduled, he felt a tug; and he had himself under enough control by the time he reached the fifth to pull in. As he stepped down out of the truck into an alleyway, he heard the first siren. He was supposed to be on the other side of the river by this time. He swiftly lit two of the incendiary grenades, pitched them through windows, and ran to the truck. Eldert eased the *BUSY* truck up almost to Elston so he could see passing traffic, but he kept his lights off and pulled close to the curb. His breathing was quick, his heart jumping. The siren was very near, and Eldert thought he could hear another, farther away. A sedan came by with siren and lights going, a Fire Department car headed to where Eldert had been, moving much less swiftly than the siren would lead one to expect. Eldert did not pull away from the curb because the other siren was coming near. A fire truck appeared and rattled by, going in the same direction the car had gone. Now Eldert heard other sirens in the distance. He switched the lights on, pulled the *BUSY* truck out onto nearly deserted Elston, breathed deeply, and forced himself to resume his route. The schedule was demolished, but Eldert would hold to the route. At least for now.

He finished his run down the west side of the "U," with the sounds of sirens becoming a choir of harpies. As Eldert crossed the bridge over the North Branch, he glanced up the river to his left and saw a reddish glow. It's all coming apart, he thought. Now everybody will be looking out their windows and coming out in the streets.

Not all of Eldert's fortune was bad. The stopping places he had chosen on the east side of the river could be seen from few houses, and there were no pedestrians on the back streets or in the alleys—no one out strolling in gale-force winds at 1:00 A.M. But the wind tortured and tired Eldert, and the sirens and the red glow growing in the sky would not quit nagging him, reminding him that he had surely run out of time. Again and again, Eldert missed what had seemed childishly easy throws. Each miss encouraged the next; a night raider does not do his best work while standing in a brilliant light. Twice he lost control of himself and threw wildly, again and again, without aiming. Eldert first noticed he was running short of grenades when he was only halfway up the east side of his "U," and he decided he would make only a few more throws and escape. He steered the *BUSY* truck into a narrow brick-paved alley and was agreeably surprised at the extent to which the buildings along it acted as a windbreak, damped down the noise, and hid him and his truck; he was in a welcome haven for the moment, and he managed a tight smile and relaxed a bit. He made a swift check of his arsenal. *No*, it can't *be*! Only eight grenades left, hardly enough for the buildings down on the south side, and he still had several buildings to do up here yet. He looked around helplessly, half expecting to see the missing silver balls lying around in the alley, half knowing that he had just thrown them away. The despair passed, and Eldert made a decision: Do as good a job as possible here, *then* worry about the south side. He took up two of the silver-colored balls and ignition devices and stepped down into the alley. One grenade was to go up there, onto the roof, the other into the ground-floor window over there. First the window. Eldert knew that the siren he heard now had to be on *this* side of the North Branch. His stomach tightened again, and his heart raced. He made the throw through the window with much more force than was needed, then ran back to the spot where he was to throw to the roof and looked up. The sky was getting eerily bright. Eldert made a practice motion with his arm. Protected from the wind, it should be an easy throw, he knew, but recent errors had eroded his confidence. Eldert made an accurate throw and cried out with pleasure. He turned and was starting for the truck when a crash close behind him froze his movement. He heard a faint rattling noise and saw the brilliant light go by his legs. The ball had somehow rolled off the roof and fallen, narrowly missing Eldert, and was rolling in the alley. He felt sweet relief. For a moment. Then alarm. The dazzling, spitting ball of light was close to the truck—*too* close. The heat of one of those balls could ignite almost *anything*. Eldert felt panic. He cast around frantically for some object to use to knock the thing away from where it lay at the rear of the truck. He tried to lift an old galvanized metal trash can, but it was too heavy to move easily. He shoved the can over and it fell heavily onto the alley, spilling out some of its load of what looked like ashes. Eldert grabbed the can near the bottom and hauled it over, freeing it of the rest of its contents. He lifted the can and ran to the rear of the truck and tried to use the can to swipe the light away. He hit something, but the light didn't move. He swung the can frantically, but the rear bumper and a tire protected the source of the dazzling light. Eldert threw the can into the air, giving no thought to whether someone might hear the sounds of the can crashing and sliding down the alley. *Tools!* Eldert remembered the tools in the back of the *BUSY* truck. He was afraid to pull the rear door of the truck open because it was so near the fizzing light that something inside the truck might be ignited. So he raced around to the front of the truck, scrambled up onto the front seat—and saw the simple solution: He merely started the truck and drove it off the light.

Eldert stopped the truck forty feet away, looked in the rear-view mirror, saw that the light had stayed put when the truck moved. He let out all the breath in his lungs and sagged on the seat. *Close* one, he told himself. Eldert's relief was short-lived. He smelled the problem before he saw it.

It was a terrific dream. He was in this contest. All the other contestants were these *young* guys—lots younger than he—and they all looked alike, *exactly* alike: like Michelangelo's *"David"* except that they had enormous peckers. The judges of the contest were all women, and one of the judges was really beautiful, made the others look plain by comparison. Well, while they were presenting the trophy to one of the Davids, this beautiful judge came over to Vernon Hooker. She was crying a little, and she told him *he* should have won; she said that, although he was pretty old and his pecker was smaller than average, the thing *he* had—

Hooker had been asleep only about an hour when his wife shook him awake and handed him the telephone. It was Benedetto, calling to say he'd be right over to pick Hooker up. "For Jesus Christ, *why?*" Hooker snapped. "Why would you want to do a shitty thing like *that?*" Benedetto hung up.

Minutes later, as Hooker climbed into the passenger side, he said sheepishly, "Good to see you, Dom."

Eldert Maddox drove east much faster than he had driven in rehearsal, but in rehearsal, he hadn't had a tire on fire. He would be driving even faster—he was sorely tempted to *floor* it—if not for the fear of attracting too much attention and for fear of losing control of the *BUSY* truck if the smoking tire burst. The wind, which was flying south and slamming into the left side of the truck, actually helped in a way, helped by carrying away the acrid smoke that poured off the burning tire and making it less obvious to the people he passed.

As he fled, Eldert debated about whether to drive into Lincoln Park when he reached it, *if* he reached it. This time of night, the park would be a place to hide and rest for a while, but if the park was as dry as everything else, there'd be a risk of the burning tire setting the park on fire. Eldert Maddox didn't give a rat's ass about the park, but he needed time, time to get rid of the burning tire, time to put the spare in its place, time to calm his nerves. Everything would be so simple, Eldert thought, if only he had a fire extinguisher, but he had never had one on this truck. Probably every other *BUSY* truck had one, he thought—at least one—but not this truck; this one was never equipped for putting fires *out*.

Eldert was spared his decision about driving the smoldering tire into Lincoln Park; the tire burst, and Eldert felt the left side go mushy. He pumped the brake and brought the truck to a controlled stop, felt the left rear of the truck settle down too low. He unlatched the door, used his left foot to help push the door open against the force of the wind, and climbed out. The tire was partly shredded but still on the rim, still smoking. Eldert got back into the truck quickly. It would be just his luck tonight, he thought, to have some fucking Good Samaritan stop. He needed a quiet side street or some other fairly level paved area. Maybe a parking lot. He shifted into first and eased forward. The park was still blocks away, and Eldert didn't want to go one foot farther than he had to. He limped along until he drew opposite a side street, stopped, and looked down it. Houses along both sides, some kind of bigger building down at the end. Most of the dwellings dark. Not bad. He backed the *BUSY* truck up a few feet, made a right turn into the side street, and drove only a few truck lengths away from the intersection before stopping in the middle of the street. He considered turning the truck around so he'd be in a better position in case he should need to get out of here in a hurry, but he decided he wasn't going to get far like this anyway, and besides, he wanted the poisonous-smelling smoke from the tire blowing *away* from him. He switched the engine off, struggled down out of the truck, and trotted around to the rear. He unloaded a platform jack and jockeyed it under the rear axle. He began to pump the jack up but remembered that he had to loosen the nuts that held the wheel on before raising the wheel off the pavement. He found the tire tool, crouched down by the burning tire, and went to work on the nuts, holding his breath as the foul black smoke tried to hide the nuts from him and tried to hurt his eyes. While Eldert was thus engaged, he did not hear the man come up behind him.

Benedetto and Hooker drove north to see if "their" buildings were involved. It was a trip into hell. A hell colored red and yellow and orange and crimson and pink and purple and amber. And nearly as bright as day. A hell so hot it left blisters where air patted skin. A hell that smelled like scorched garbage. And sounded like falling walls. And wriggled like terrified people. And looked like silhouettes of firemen doubled over to vomit.

"*Use some help?*" shouted the man behind Eldert.

Eldert jumped spastically. He whirled around, still in a crouch, still gripping the wheel wrench, and looked up at a smiling man in a white T-shirt and khaki pants. Eldert stood up warily. The man was several inches shorter than Eldert. The man had to be at least sixty; his hair was white; and he had a belly like a woman seven, eight months "gone." Nevertheless, he gave an unmistakable impression of fitness. He looked like a man who worked with his body, then went fishing or bowling and laughed often.

"My *God!*" Eldert shouted, to be heard above the sound of the wind. "You scared the *shit* out of me!"

The man laughed and asked Eldert about the smoldering tire. Eldert told the white-haired man that he

• 152 •

had tried to help some folks back there—Eldert held out a gloved hand in the direction of the rising red glow to the west of them—and that his tire had caught fire.

"What was hot enough to start a *tire*?" the man wanted to know.

Eldert made a you've-got-me shrug and said, "All kinds of industrial stuff's burning back there." Eldert added that he had to get back there to help people out, and he offered the man fifty dollars to help him change the tire quickly.

By way of answer, the white-haired man grinned and held out his hand for the wheel wrench. Eldert gave it to him, and the man set to work loosening the lug nuts.

Eldert didn't even want to think about it. This man had seen him under circumstances the man would not be likely to forget, circumstances that absolutely linked Eldert and his *BUSY* truck to the fires. It was dark here, but Eldert was sure that this man had gotten too good a look at his face. But what the hell was Eldert to do? Stand out here and murder this guy in the street? The man was apparently no immediate threat—certainly Eldert could get away from him now, once the tire was changed—but afterward—

"O-o-*kay!*" shouted the white-haired man, and Eldert jumped again.

"Sorry," said the man. And then, as if to minimize blame for his offense: "You're really nervous."

This is getting worse and worse, thought Eldert. "I'm tired," he said dismissively. "Long shift."

Eldert pumped the jack up quickly. The *BUSY* truck shuddered in the wind, but it stayed up on the jack. While the white-haired man backed the nuts off the lug bolts and dropped them into the hubcap, Eldert pulled a spade and a long wrecking bar out of the truck. Eldert handed the spade to the white-haired man, and working together, the two men pulled the burning wheel off the lug bolts and let it fall to the street. Then they pushed and pulled the smoking wheel to the gutter several feet from the truck. The white-haired man turned abruptly, strode to the back of the truck, and shoved the spade inside. In the several seconds this took, Eldert tried to think of a good excuse to stop him, tried to *tell* him to stop, but he only stammered, and it was lost in the wind. The white-haired man leaned inside the truck for what seemed to Eldert to be minutes—would he see the silver-colored balls, the ignition devices, and wonder what they were, *suspect* what they were?—and came out with the spare, bounced it on the street, and rolled it to the waiting Eldert. The two men lifted the wheel up onto the lug bolts. The white-haired man squatted down eagerly and began picking the lug nuts up out of the hubcap, one by one, and spinning them onto the bolts, then tightening them only as much as he could with his short, stubby fingers. When the man looked up and nodded, Eldert let the jack down, then picked the jack up and loaded in onto the truck. Eldert peered around the corner of the truck and saw the man had begun to use the wrench to tighten the lug nuts. Working quickly, Eldert clutched the spade and moved around behind the squatting figure. He scanned the dark street for possible witnesses, saw no one. If someone was standing at a dark window and watching them right now, Eldert speculated, someone awakened by the wind or the sirens, that witness could probably read the *BUSY,* probably could *not* read the license plate, and almost certainly could not identify Eldert's face. Eldert's heart was racing, and his knees began to tremble. He felt cold and sick. He had to do it—*right now,* he told himself. He gripped the handle of the spade with both hands. But hesitated; he just stood there and watched the man testing his weight and strength against the last nut. Then the realization hit Eldert: You've waited too long, he told himself, and his panic leaped. But instead of getting up, the white-haired man was looking around for something: the hubcap. He found it and lined it up in preparation for forcing it into place. Eldert had time to, time to—

Clank! and *clank!* again; the hubcap went home.

Thwuunk! and *thwuunk!* again; the white-haired man would never go home.

Eldert snatched up the wheel wrench but dropped it before he got to the rear of the truck. He retrieved the wrench and threw it into the back of the truck, hitting his shin painfully with the spade as he did. As Eldert got both the spade and himself aboard and fumbled with the ignition key, his mind and heart were racing so wildly that each moment seemed to play out in incredibly slow motion, and each moment was costing him. He got the engine started, got the vehicle into reverse gear, stepped on the accelerator, and backed the truck around the corner. Then he shifted to drive and stomped on the gas pedal. Loose objects in the back of the truck made angry noises. The *BUSY* truck ran east until Eldert drove it into the park and found a dark place to stop.

Eldert's body was not working right. His stomach hurt. He felt weak. He had a peculiar bitter taste in his mouth. He sat in the park for a while and watched something else that wasn't working right: Dawn was coming at 2:00 A.M., and it was breaking in the *west*.

———

The Red Wind marched on the North Side in a formation three belts deep. Along the leading edge—in a belt half a dozen blocks wide—scores of buildings were already smoking, though they had not yet been touched by fire. Dinner heating up for the Red Wind. Even half a mile from the flames, windows grew too hot to touch. Living things that had not escaped began to die. In the blocks nearest the fire, buildings burst into flames, tar on the streets puddled and burned, and railroad spurs curled up into the air, sometimes into crooked letter "o's."

The middle belt was a crematory. Temperatures were so high that the chemical reactions of burning were taking place millions of times faster than they would at room temperature. Nothing could remain standing; it either went down to ashes or was sucked up into the air as steam or smoke, or as burning debris to be thrown out in front.

In the rear belt, where most of the fuel had been consumed, smaller fires were left behind to burn themselves out.

And behind *this* lay a growing black wake that, save for the wind, was curiously quiet.

The wind larruping the building. Sirens. Balcony doors sliding. People shouting. Hammond had been awakened by the sounds before the phone rang in the short, insistent b-r-rings of the Enter-Phone. It was the night doorman, George, to say that there was some kind of fire to the west and that tenants were being notified to evacuate. Instructions from the police were to be calm, don't use the phone except for life-and-death emergencies, leave now, stay close to the lake, and forget possessions—just *go*. Did the chief need some help? Hammond told the doorman he didn't think so;

he would try to drive his own car. Hammond asked if any part of *this* building was on fire. No. Is any adjacent building on fire? No, Chief. How near is the fire? People say a mile, about, maybe more. Hammond thanked the doorman and hung up.

He dialed the number for the Communications Center. Busy. He tried the Academy, listened to two rings, then heard a crisp answer: "Fire Academy."

"This is Chief Hammond. Who's this?"

"Chief! Boogelewski, sir."

"Oh, yes, Boogelewski." Right job for him, thought Hammond: night duty in an empty, locked-up building. "What's going on there?"

"Well, sir, the horn is crackin' more'n I ever dreamed. Otherwise the place is a tomb."

Hammond thought about having Boogelewski check for him on where the fire was and how fast it was moving in his direction, but he dismissed the idea and ended the conversation. He poled his way out through the living room and opened the sliding doors. He started out onto the balcony but felt the violence of the wind and swung back inside. He listened to sirens and tried to judge how far away they were. Several blocks at least. Hammond would have been willing to walk out of there stark naked if that were indicated; anytime there's a fire, it's no time to be vain or modest. However, he was sure there wasn't that much urgency now. He could allow himself ten minutes to get out of the building. He checked his watch: 1:15 A.M.

Hammond slid the door shut and latched it. Then *un*latched it: If a fireman wanted to come in this way, make it easy. He paddled back to the bedroom and started pulling on a uniform. He couldn't get the left pant leg over the cast. There was no time; he threw the trousers in the direction of the door and swiftly dressed, hat and all, except that he had neither sock nor shoe on the left foot—and no pants. He checked his shorts for holes, then pushed keys and cigarettes into his shirt pocket. Hammond did not need to think about what things to save. He knew the lesson: Few things are very important when there's a fire. He grabbed the notes and the partial manuscript for his latest book, threw his trousers over a shoulder, and went out, not taking time for what might be a last look. He heard his telephone ringing, but he closed the door. He left the door unlocked and paddled off down the hall.

There were friends who would take him in. Hotels. Hammond's thoughts turned to his second home: the Academy.

He pushed the down button and waited for three minutes for one of the elevators to stop at the sixth floor. As he waited, Hammond considered with growing dread the prospect of descending four flights of stairs on these goddamn crutches, to where his car was parked on the second floor. Just as he had decided that it was time for the stairs, he heard a *ding!* and saw a light switch on. Below the light, a set of elevator doors slid open. The car had come up from the lobby with just one passenger aboard. Hammond was surprised to see the passenger, and the passenger was surprised to see this tall man in the full uniform of the Chicago Fire Department—except that he had no pants.

"Je-sus Ch-*rist!*" said Dominic Benedetto. "Haven't I seen enough tonight without having to look at *this?*"

Most fires are like zoo cats, approachable with caution only if they are small or under control. But the Red Wind was loose, and it looked in windows on the twentieth floor. It took a block of houses in one mouthful and spit out plumbing like chicken bones. The Red Wind was ravening, and a fire out of control is a killing creature.

The Red Wind killed with poison gases. With carbon monoxide: odorless and invisible carbon monoxide; it goes into your blood, takes the oxygen, robs you of judgment, then kills you. With phosgene, the dreaded gas of World War I, long outlawed but so easily produced by burning one of the most common plastics. And with hydrogen cyanide, the same gas used to execute convicted murderers. Formaldehyde. And more than a hundred other toxic gases.

The Red Wind killed with blasts of superheated air, which felled people and glued their lungs together.

With smoke, which hid exits and bewildered.

With flames, which made people leap out of windows and which so completely consumed some of the bodies that no traces would be found.

The Red Wind killed by competing with people for the oxygen in the surrounding atmosphere. Where the oxygen concentration fell below 16 percent, people found it difficult to think, felt so-o-o tired, couldn't get their hands and their legs to behave: their attempts to escape became ineffective. Where the oxygen content fell below 6 percent, they stopped breathing.

The Red Wind killed with falling walls, collapsing roofs, whole buildings doing spectacular pratfalls.

And the Red Wind killed with explosions. The explosions came in assorted sizes. Small: aerosol cans spraying metal fragments. Medium: TV tubes going—imploding, actually—with an odd sound that firemen recognized. Large: fuel tanks hurling pieces of vehicles onto roofs blocks away. Autos and trucks could not all be driven or towed away fast enough, and there was an occasional explosion that sent parts of them flying through buildings and through other vehicles. In some cases, fuel tanks were ruptured, and gasoline ran downhill—down streets and down sewers—until it was ignited, sometimes blocks away. From the point of ignition, the fire traveled on the vapors at fifteen feet per second.

The Red Wind killed and killed.

The "city with the big shoulders"—and sometimes with the open fly—has one hell of a front yard. Twelve hundred acres of precious lakefront beauty in Lincoln Park alone; all the way from North Avenue on up to Hollywood Avenue. Pressures to whack down some of the foliage in Lincoln Park because criminals can lurk there have been resisted so far because, if you're going to have a beautiful park, you're going to have some hiding places.

Thwuunk!

Eldert heard the sound in his mind. Had the spade made any sound moving through the air or just when it hit?

Thwuunk!

Eldert took a deep breath and let it out slowly, and as the breath leaked away, he closed his eyes and slowly slumped forward as if the air in his lungs were all that had held him up against the seat. He rested his forehead on the steering wheel and wondered if he would ever feel energetic again. Going to the south side and finishing his work, that seemed impossible now. He was used up. The fear had been the worst part, really. But he should be safe here in the park for a while.

Then it occurred to him: Surely there was a regular

police patrol of the park; there would have to be. It might be affected tonight by all the uproar, but he couldn't afford to bet that nobody would be coming around. He sat up and looked around. Nothing, at least nothing he could see. Suppose the police, or park police or whatever, stopped and asked him what he was doing here. What could he tell them? That he had gotten a little sick from breathing smoke over there on a job and had pulled in here to rest? That might get him by, but what would they find if they decided to take a look inside this truck? The few remaining silver-colored balls and the ignition devices. It was tempting to forget about the buildings on the south side and just get the hell out of this city. He'd already been through too much for one night. He could slip through the park and throw the balls and the ignition devices into one of the park's lagoons. Or would it be better to bury them? He could just take the spade and—the *spade*! Oh-h-h, *shit*! Just several blocks from here, there lies a guy with his head smashed in, and there's a burned tire beside him. And here *I* sit, thought Eldert, with no spare tire and with a spade that's got, that's got part of the guy's *head* on it. Eldert shivered. Suddenly the spade was menacing, *threatening* him, not alone as evidence of arson and murder; it had part of the dead man's *head* on it. He opened the door and stepped down out of the truck, closing the door quickly to make the dome light go out. He groped around the truck, pulled open the rear door, and found the spade. Reluctantly, Eldert picked the spade up by its handle, forcing his eyes not to look at the blade end of it. He carried it only a few feet away before he stopped, afraid. He saw nothing, but that didn't mean there was nothing there. In a Chicago park at night with the wind howling, there could be muggers or sex maniacs or— He flung the spade at some bushes and ran, ran back to the truck and jumped inside, frantically slamming the door shut after him to bar whatever might be pursuing him. He pushed down the locking device on the door and sat there on the truck seat, breathing hard. Eldert remembered coming home from horror movies when he was a boy. Coming home in the sunshine, he might laugh at the whole business, but coming home after dark, that was different. Walking along deserted streets, he knew that every doorway might be the one, every bush. If anything, there were more doorways now, more bushes. He started the engine, pulled out of the park, and headed south, glad to be on a street and moving.

People were not the only living things to die. With fire riding on their backs—eating their hair—dogs and cats and rats and squirrels ran until they fell, sometimes carrying the fire to fresh locations. Parakeets, canaries, and parrots were set free from their cages, but many of them—like the somewhat more independent pigeons— became confused and flew *into* the fire, and many more were sucked into it by mercurial air currents. Chicago's ubiquitous locust trees could not run or fly; they stood their ground, and by the thousands, they were consumed. And goldfish boiled in their little glass bowls, and tropical fish poached in their aquariums.

A cup of coffee. He didn't know why it sounded so good, but that's what Eldert wanted. *Craved.* But he knew he could not afford to risk a coffee stop; on a night like this, there was too great a chance he would encounter another board-up driver or an insurance executive or somebody else who might have reason to remember him or his *BUSY* truck. Later, he told himself.

He would work his way south, keeping to the lakeshore until he came to Michigan Avenue. If Eldert skipped the buildings on the south side, he could be out of the city in half an hour. Mr. Ruck would understand.

People were driving erratically because of the light in the sky. Eldert tried to concentrate on his driving—he could not afford an accident now—but his excitement was growing. He had never imagined traffic this heavy in the middle of the night. It seemed as if everything with wheels on it was rolling south, and even the sidewalks were busy.

Tomorrow, after he had rested, he could buy a Chicago paper. Every city of any size in America gets the *Tribune* or the *Sun-Times*, or both, and several communities in neighboring states receive them the same day. He would be able to sit somewhere, in sweet safety and anonymity, and read about how many buildings had actually been destroyed. Eldert guessed that it was probably a lot more than the thirty-five buildings he had planned to involve.

The main wall of fire was twenty stories high, and it rolled down both sides of the North Branch of the Chicago River, making noises like a giant waterfall. Fire fighters staggered backward, conceding block after block. And they regarded the sky over their heads with growing apprehension. A hail of burning brands and embers rode the screaming wind high over their heads, to shower down somewhere behind them; flaming debris carried aloft by chimneys of superheated air became paratroopers dropping behind enemy lines, falling on rooftops, lancing through windows, turning even "fireproof" structures into raging furnaces that held it as long as they could, then failed and spilled out their fires. The special nightmare of every fire chief became a monstrous reality: numerous fires in different locations at the same time.

―――――――――

As Eldert neared the Chicago River, he gaped. Great geysers of water filled the air over the Chicago River to a height of several stories. The fountains caught light and gave off mists for the wind to carry south. It was almost as if the bridge ran right through a giant falls. Down in the river lay three fireboats, and they were throwing up sprays to wet down buildings on both sides of the river and to hold up a curtain of water to protect the Loop from the fusillade of burning brands and embers. Eldert saw a firebrand riding the tearing wind high above the wall of water.

Eldert was flabbergasted. The city is going nuts, and *I*—

He continued south, away from the ruckus. Earlier tonight, it had seemed that his project had been botched. Some *botched,* he thought. He, *he,* had taken the great city of Chicago by the throat and was sque-e-e-zing. Suddenly it was the time of Eldert's life. He felt giddy. He regarded the magnificent buildings along both sides of him now, *arrogantly.* While Chicago is in trouble back there, he thought, I could, if I *wanted* to, burn down *any* goddamn *thing.* Christ, if you were going to burn down some buildings, would there ever be a better time than this? No, never. Eldert thought again about the buildings on the south side. While he drove down Michigan Avenue. Toward them.

Some things it consumed swiftly; it would take a woman's hair—lacquered with hair spray—in a *flash*; it broke into liquor stores and chose the 90- and 100-proof liquors. Some things it claimed more slowly; it melted stone and metal and drove the liquid into the air.

Most "fireproof" buildings were like furnaces with plenty of fuel inside, just waiting to be lit: paint and carpeting and wood paneling and ceiling tiles and furnishings and papers and merchandise of all sorts. Once the fire got inside, it usually found plenty to eat.

The trick with "fireproof" buildings was getting in, but the Red Wind might just as well have had the keys. Early in the spread of the fire—before gas and electricity were shut off to reduce explosions—innumerable air-conditioning systems were running on this hot night. Rapidly, efficiently, they had helped to spread smoke, poisonous gases, and explosive vapors throughout the structures. Combustible vapors spread out and prowled the buildings till they found something with a hot wire or a flame—a range, water heater, constant-on TV or intercom, elevator motor, exhaust fan, refrigerator, *something*. A flame wasn't even necessary if a room could be heated hot enough to get something inside the room smoking. Once the Red Wind got its growth, many "fireproof" buildings were breached by the simple expedient of toppling one building over on another, that building spilling on yet another, and so on. Flaming boards burst through windows. Showers of sparks landed on roofs. Burning debris landed in partly open parking areas on lower floors.

Even if walls and floors were made of fireproof materials, there were usually plenty of "flues." Horizontal flues: corridors, spaces above suspended ceilings, utility conduits, air-conditioning ducts. And vertical flues: stairwells, elevator shafts, utility shafts.

And once the Red Wind began to march in triumph, sprinkler systems and streams from firemen's hoses could merely slow it; they couldn't stop it. The raging fire turned much of the water to vapor, causing many fire fighters to wonder how much of their seemingly dinky streams were even *getting* there. In a few cases, water thrown at the Red Wind even proved *detrimental*— as it was in the case of a four-story paper storage warehouse; the water did not put the fire out, but it did cause the contents to swell up in volume until the walls were pushed out—and fell on fire-fighting equipment.

The exposed steelwork holding up some of the buildings turned sissy in the heat. It couldn't help it; unprotected steel lost strength as its temperature increased; by the time it reached eight hundred degrees, it had lost 90 percent of its ability to stand. Some buildings twisted—it seemed to onlookers that they *writhed* in the heat—before they fell.

"Ol' Hooker's had himself quite a night. This woman comes runnin' up with 'er dress on fire, and ol' Hooks, he just steps up and tears it right *off* 'er."

At this point, Benedetto illustrated his narrative with a violent sweep of his right hand to show Hammond something of Hooker's dress-tearing technique. Benedetto was pleased to see the startled look on Hammond's face—which, in reality, was a reaction not to Benedetto's story but rather to the fact of Benedetto's taking his one usable hand off the steering wheel while driving south at close to forty miles per hour.

To the drillmaster's considerable relief, the policeman clamped his big hand back on the wheel and resumed his story. "Slick as you please. He packs 'er off in the wagon, and I shake his hand. Well, when I take 'is hand, he makes a face. I look at 'is hands and they're all burned, I mean *cooked*. He bitched all the way to the emergency ward. Made me promise to pick 'im up in an hour so he could get back to work; otherwise he would not go in the goddamn hospital. The old sonofa*bitch*," Benedetto said in an admiring tone, as if he were talking about a son. "He was gonna *defy* me. So, after I drop you at the Academy, I gotta go back and pick the bonehead up." Clearly that errand was not one that Benedetto considered a burden.

Fire-fighting units were called out in groups. As each additional alarm was struck, units hopscotched from outlying stations to points nearer and nearer the fire, then rushed into combat. When it became plain that the conflagration was, in fact, not one fire but several, calls for help were rifled to other cities.

A dark sedan waited in Grant Park—engine running, man in the driver's seat, pointed west so the man could pull out onto Michigan Avenue in a hurry. The headlights were off, but little amber lights mounted on the fenders blinked: caution—caution—caution.

Ask the man what he did—what he was doing here tonight, in fact—and he'd tell you he was a news photographer. However, his credentials as a news photographer were skimpy. Besides the blinking amber lights, there were two signs on the sedan, one on the outside of each front door, which said PRESS PHOTOGRAPHER. The signs clipped on, held against the doors by little magnets (and clipped *off* when his wife rode in the car; this was their only car, and Idas made him take the signs off before she would ride in it). On the front seat, beside the driver, were the tools: a big press camera and an electronic scanner radio. And in the driver's pocket was his *Daily News* card. It had his name, Jules Aroni, on it; it had a picture of Aroni, taken when he had hair, and it said that Aroni was, indeed, a press photographer. Only thing was, the *Daily News* had folded—died of a circulation problem, Aroni liked to say—in 1978. By then, Aroni had been a newspaper photographer for forty-one years, and he decided he was getting too old to make the jump to one of the remaining papers. So he retired and stayed home with Idas. For nine days. He didn't have the kind of marriage that makes you want twin beds with a moat full of crocodiles between them— Idas wasn't like that—but Aroni needed something to do. He had decided to become a free-lance photographer, sell pictures to newspapers, maybe even an occasional magazine. So Aroni got the secondhand press camera, the amber lights that would blink, the magnetic signs, the scanner radio. Mostly, he got his leads by listening to the scanner. It blinked little red lights as it patrolled radio frequencies used by police and fire services in the field. When the scanner picked up a transmission, it would automatically stop at that channel and let Aroni eavesdrop on the message.

In his years as a free-lancer, Jules Aroni had sold few pictures—mostly what they call "human interest" stuff— but he did not complain. What the hell, he told himself, it didn't take many sales to pay for the gas and the film.

And it didn't take many sales to keep you from feeling like just another old fart with no place to go.

And there was something else: a sense of anticipation. Whenever he was listening to his scanner, waiting for a clue that might lead him to a newsworthy photo, Aroni felt excitement. Sort of like fishing; maybe you hadn't had a decent bite in weeks, but there was still that chance that something big might hit in the very next second. And on a night like this, anything was possible. Hell, tonight you could get a wire-service photo. So Aroni waited for a message. He didn't know what message, didn't even know what it would be *about*, but he hoped he could recognize it when he heard it.

Aroni looked at his watch: two thirty-two. He switched off the automatic scanning device so that he could manually select one channel, then another. There was so much radio traffic tonight, so many emergency channels in use at once, that he could listen to only a fraction of it. Christ, the city was shaking. Aroni had been up on the north side, had been caught in human torrents, had been shooed away by policemen and firemen, had gotten propositions and threats from people who wanted his auto, and had even taken a few pictures. Unsalable pictures, he was sure. The area was absolutely teeming with newsmen. Aroni was certain a couple of the pictures he had shot had other photographers in them—probably caught at the moment they were taking pictures with *other* photographers in *them*. So he had decided to come down here and wait along Michigan Avenue, listening to emergency messages. The maelstrom was moving this way. He was near public offices. Maybe down here he could breathe some air, could get to something without a building falling on his car, maybe get a picture without three other photographers in it. No sense in just wasting film.

No sense in wasting gas either. Aroni switched off the

engine. He sat facing the traffic streaming along Michigan Avenue—people rolling to his right, toward the light, and people rolling to his left, refugees running before the Red Wind. Aroni listened to the transmissions pouring out of his radio. He paid no special attention to the *BUSY* truck as it rolled down Michigan Avenue, to his left.

As the fire bore down on them, some people performed acts that were without point or purpose. A shopkeeper, who ran out of his store after the roof burst into flames, paused long enough to lock the front door, then tried the knob to make sure it was locked securely. An old woman who could see the fire approaching her bungalow, scurried about inside changing linens and tidying up.

People gambled lives, their own and others', in ignoble ways. Thousands remained as close to the Red Wind as they could stand to be, to loot. Others fought with one another over property that would end up burning anyway. Some dropped possessions out of upper-story windows and hit people who happened to be passing below. Many more lugged their possessions out into streets and parkings lots and parks and then abandoned them—where they became convenient stepping-stones to help the fire run across the open areas. In front of the Red Wind, every street became a Babel; gigantic entanglements of people—drivers asking astronomical sums, muggers and thieves, the curious who came to rubberneck—clotted the streets and made passage of emergency vehicles difficult. Many reacted to the crisis by quickly drinking themselves into a stupor. Some took too long to find clothing to cover their bodies "properly" before leaving burning buildings. Others risked their necks to save possessions that could have been replaced for a week's wages, even a day's. A man carrying a TV set or a woman wearing three fur coats could not run far without tiring. People streaming away from the Red Wind with their most valuable possessions were such sweet and tempting targets that muggers—quite unprepared for this Niagara of opportunity—sometimes felt burdened by the need to make so many decisions. People fled in mindless panic, some running down other people, some confused by fire reflected in windows and turning the wrong way.

But there were other people too. People who buried a few possessions in the ground or just walked away from their things without looking back. People who went out naked and were not ashamed. And people who honored life: rescuing, protecting, calming.

Hammond laid a hand on Benedetto's shoulder and said, "*No, no.*" Benedetto braked sharply. The massive policeman had started to drive the sedan right up onto the pedestrian plaza that lies before the front entrance to the Fire Academy. Jesus! "This is far enough."

As the drillmaster worked his way out and up onto his crutches, Benedetto said, "Chief, do somethin', willya? Rosewater's still at the County Buildin'. Phone 'im, tell 'im to look for me. Soon's I get Hooks, I'll swing past and get 'im. Tell 'im the Randolph Street side, okay? An' get some pants on, fer Chrissakes."

Hammond poled his way across the concrete-and-brick-paved plaza. The duty man, "Boogaloo" Boogelewski saw Hammond approaching the glass-enclosed lobby and held the door open. Boogelewski was delighted to see the drillmaster more or less on his feet and he said so, but the statement was brief and carefully formal, in deference to Hammond's rank. Hammond began to work his way across the lobby toward his ground-floor office, but he stopped before a set of alarm devices—a tapping key, a speaker, and a tape puncher—that were chattering about disaster on a monstrous scale.

Boogelewski, who had relocked the front door and come up behind the drillmaster, said softly, "Started a little after I came on at midnight, Chief. Been goin' like a pinball machine since about twelve-thirty."

Hammond labored into his office and sat behind his so-familiar desk. He had been away from here just one week, but everything that had happened before that week now seemed oddly remote.

Hammond told Boogelewski to get on the phone to track down Police Sergeant Dennis Rosewater at the County Building for him.

"Yes, *sir!*" Boogelewski spun and hurried—*trotted*—out to his glass-partitioned office.

Hammond watched the retreating back and felt a surge of emotion. The man looked so goddamn frail, and his uniform was too big for him. Boogelewski was wasting away, literally shrinking. Personnel at the Academy were not fooled by Boogelewski's disguise—his dyed hair, jaunty moustache, tinted glasses, his feigned vigor; they were sure the man was dying. Boogelewski was a veteran who had breathed too much smoke and who could have retired, several years ago, as disabled. But "Boogaloo" Boogelewski was a fireman; the most important thing in his life was *being* a fireman, not having *been* one; and, thanks to Hammond and a couple of other officers, he was able to remain a fireman. And Boogaloo will soon die a fireman, Hammond thought, and it occurred to Hammond that there were worse epitaphs.

Boogelewski reappeared in Hammond's doorway to say that he had Sergeant Rosewater on the line. Hammond picked up the receiver and passed along Benedetto's message. Hammond was about to terminate the conversation when it occurred to him to ask Rosewater, "Find anything useful?"

"Yes, sir," Rosewater replied. "I think so. We just finished working over an area on the near south side, and we found three more deeds—all to trust departments and all with the mailing address of the same attorney on them. According to the assessment records, what we've got are three industrial buildings along Indiana Avenue."

"You have a car there?" said Hammond.

"No, sir. You want me to try to get one, Chief?"

"No, I guess not. No, give me the addresses of those three buildings and wait there for Benedetto."

Hammond wrote down the south side addresses, then hung up and sat at his desk and told himself it wouldn't hurt to wait. But he didn't believe it. He summoned Boogelewski and gave him the name of a police officer, a man he knew well from his years as an arson investigator. In less than a minute, Boogelewski had the man on the line. Hammond asked the policeman if it would be possible to have a squad car swing by some buildings on Indiana and check on them. Hammond gave him the three addresses and added that if there was a *BUSY* truck in that neighborhood, the driver should be considered potentially dangerous and should be detained. The policeman agreed to have it done as soon as the work load would permit and to get back to Hammond when he could. Hammond hung up and wondered how long that might take on a crazy night like this.

Check the fuel gauge: three quarters of a tank. Check the time: two thirty-eight. Directed by gloved hands, the *BUSY* truck turned onto Indiana Avenue and crept up the street. Eldert hunched over the wheel, looking for signs of life. He saw none; the street was deserted. He eased the truck over and stopped it in front of a five-story building. He switched the engine off and stepped down into the street, into the tearing wind. Still no one about.

Eldert hastily regarded the buildings to be burned. He had planned to set at least ten or twelve buildings afire, but he had only six grenades left. Well, if he used just one grenade for each building, he could still get three decoy buildings. The southernmost of the decoy buildings were out. The way the wind was howling down Indiana Avenue, the fire would probably get 'em anyway. It would work if he made every grenade count; he couldn't afford any more misses. The way the wind was slamming this way, then that, Eldert knew he couldn't risk any demanding throws—no third-story or roof shots. The tough nut would be that monster in the middle: a massive old five-story brick loft with corrugated plastic panels over the window openings on the first three floors. Should he skip it, hope the wind would carry the fire to it? No, Eldert decided; it's one of "our" buildings, it's the biggest, and there are no wall openings at all on the sides next to the other buildings. And it was full of paper boxes: a tempting target. The double-hung windows on the fourth and fifth floors were large, but so were the expanses of brick wall between them. Eldert couldn't be sure of an accurate throw in this wind, and you sure as hell didn't get more than one try with each of these grenades. Besides, the lower he could place that one grenade that was going into each building, the better. Force the door? Eldert judged he could do it easily with the extra-long wrecking bar he carried in the *BUSY* truck. Burglar alarm? No bell box on the front of the building, where it was most likely to be. Silent alarm? Probably not for an old warehouse full of paper boxes, but you couldn't be sure. Eldert quickly ticked off the steps. He'd work from downwind to upwind, starting with that south building there with the mesh on the windows. He'd take wire cutters and two balls, run down the street, snip an opening in the mesh and toss in a grenade, hit the second building, and dash back here. He'd grab what he needed, pop the door on the big one, and get the ball in. Then he'd get back to the truck and drive up to the last three buildings. Eldert was feeling strong again, pumped up.

Hammond considered sending Boogelewski. Boogelewski, whose clothes seemed to get a little bigger each night while he slept. Boogelewski, who didn't know the first thing about this case.

"You have a car here?" Hammond asked.

"No, *sir!*" said the dying fireman. "Wife brought me."

"Call next door," said Hammond, referring to the active fire station adjacent to the Academy. "See what vehicles they have there now."

Boogelewski made the call and was back standing in the doorway to Hammond's office in less than one minute. He told Hammond that all of the rolling stock normally stationed there was gone. Only one truck was there now, that brought up from Blue Island, to cover.

"That old rescue truck on the drill yard," Hammond said. "Will that thing run?"

"Far as I know, Chief. Yes, sir."

Hammond said, "See if it'll start, and if it will, bring it up to the back door."

"Yes, *sir*!" Boogelewski said and trotted off.

Hammond heard the sound of the wind come up briefly as Boogelewski went through an outside door. The hostile sound poked a hole in Hammond's quiet resolve, but the chink was quickly covered over. Even if that old truck would start, the chances of trouble at that Indiana Avenue location were slight. Besides, even if there *were* trouble there, Hammond didn't have to get involved actively; he could simply observe and call for help. The *real* problem was driving with one foot, but traffic down here—this far away from the fire up on the north side—and at this time of night should be slight, and he could drive slowly. If it was too tough, he could simply give it up. Hammond was at once aware that he had no business making this run and that he was going to do it anyway.

He waited. It was night-quiet except for the sounds of the wind outside and the racket of the Marshall System out in the lobby. He thought about the firemen trying to stop this thing. And he thought about Sheri Sue. And about a circus-size fat man named Sid Ruck.

The howl of the wind got louder for a moment as Boogelewski came in. The cadaverous fireman reported to the drillmaster that the truck was running and had almost half a tank. "You want me to drive somewheres, Chief?"

Hammond told him no, that Boogelewski was to remain at his post and that the truck was for Hammond, to take a ride over to Indiana Avenue to look at some buildings that might possibly be the targets of an arsonist. Hammond saw the look come on Boogelewski's face and held up a hand to bar the words of concern.

Hammond gave Boogelewski the addresses of the three Indiana Avenue buildings, told him to get in touch with Benedetto's car at once, give Benedetto the addresses, and tell Benedetto that Hammond was on his way there and would meet Benedetto there. Hammond instructed Boogelewski to ask that the message be radioed directly to Benedetto, complete with the addresses; Hammond wanted to avoid the delays that might result if Benedetto were requested to switch to one of the confidential frequencies, which were overloaded tonight, or to the alternative of requesting Benedetto to phone in for a confidential message. Hammond also told Boogelewski to try to locate Rosewater again at the County Building to give him the same instructions in case Benedetto's car could not be reached promptly for some reason. When it was clear to Hammond that Boogelewski understood his instructions, Hammond pushed back his desk chair, got up onto his crutches, and began poling his way toward the door to the drill yard.

———————

Eldert drew out the long wrecking bar and laid it under the truck. Then he lifted out one silver-colored ball and an ignition device and laid them on the pavement, next to the bar. Then a flashlight. These were the things Eldert would be needing for his assault on the five-story building, and when he came dashing back from the first two buildings, he'd want them in a hurry.

Eldert shoved a pair of wire cutters into a back pocket, picked up two of the silver-colored balls, and ran. To the south building. Set the balls down. Wire cutters. Snip screening. Back into pocket. Pull wire back. Not cut enough. More snipping. Sweat coming. *There.* Back into pocket. Wire pulling away easily. Pick up one ball. *Throw.* Noise of glass breaking, blown away on the yowling wind. Other ball; quick, pick it up. Run against the wind, thirty paces to the second building. Best place? Set. Hard throw. Run back to truck. Hard to make ground against the wind.

Eldert was concentrating on the work, driving out fear. Squatting down beside the truck, he shoved the flashlight into a back pocket, felt it hit the wire cutters, hoped he hadn't broken the flashlight. He picked up the long wrecking bar and the silver-colored ball and hurried the few paces to the pedestrian door in the front elevation of the five-story warehouse. He laid the ball down on a strip of gravel edging the sidewalk so he could have both hands free to work the bar. He shoved the sharp edge on one end of the tool into the small crack between the face of the door and the door frame and then pulled the opposite end of the bar away from the door—back toward himself—*hard.* The sharp end of the bar slipped out of the frame, and Eldert, off balance and pushed by the wind, let go of the bar and took several small steps backward to avoid being struck by it. Eldert was bending down to retrieve the tool when he became aware of moving lights: an approaching car. Eldert slipped to the ground, scrabbled up against the warehouse, and watched. An auto. Light rack on top. Blue and white, *police car.* Coming along the street slowly, approaching the *BUSY* truck from the rear. The police car kept moving until it came to the truck, then stopped alongside. A spotlight was switched on and turned on the truck. The patrol car was backed up, and the light was maneuvered onto the back of the truck. Eldert was relieved that he had not left the truck idling or its doors open. He shifted his elbows, turning enough without getting out of his prone position to look south, toward the two buildings he had already hit; but from this position, Eldert couldn't see them. Somehow, the cop had apparently missed the damaged windows and the incipient fires, but in another minute or two, he *couldn't* miss them. Eldert turned back to watch the patrol car and saw that the spotlight had been turned off. However, the patrol car just sat there. Precious seconds were ticking away. *Move;* Eldert willed the car to *move.* The door on the driver's side was pushed open, and a uniformed officer struggled up out of the patrol car. Most of the way out. Then he climbed back inside quickly and sat for a moment, his door still open, his left foot on the street. Then the foot swung inside, the door was pulled shut, and the patrol car started to *move.* The car sprang ahead, and the siren and blinking lights were going before the car turned off Indiana less than a block away.

———————

Hammond rode with blinking lights going but no siren, and he tried to fight back the growing conviction that he was a fool. What the hell did he think he was trying to do? Well, if he *was* a fool on a fool's errand, he certainly had fitting transportation. This toothless and gutless red dinosaur was a vehicle for *pretend* fires. Of late, whenever one of its vital organs had gone bad or whenever one was needed for transplant to some younger truck, it was simply taken in a crude surgical procedure. One of these procedures, Hammond noted, had been a radioectomy. Hammond was driving awkwardly because of the cast. When he came to north–south streets and to other open areas, blasts of wind hit the red truck and made it shudder. He was getting farther and farther from any place he belonged, and he knew he ought to turn back. He thought of the shotgun he had left behind, lying beside his bed.

Benedetto replaced the microphone so violently it bounced back off its perch and fell to the floor. *"That crazy sonofabitch!"* he yelled. He hit the siren and tromped on the accelerator so hard that Hooker's and Rosewater's heads popped back.

The radio message was also heard by someone closer to their destination: an old man sitting in a dark sedan with blinking amber lights and signs that said PRESS PHOTOGRAPHER. That could be *it,* thought Jules Aroni, and he reached for the ignition key.

There was no time to jubilate now. Eldert scrambled to his feet and renewed his assault. Popping the door and getting the grenade in took less than two minutes. Eldert sprinted back to the *BUSY* truck, wrenched the door open, and lunged inside. He started the engine, shifted to drive, and pulled ahead for half a block. This time he left the engine idling. He lifted two silver-colored balls, one in each gloved hand. As he climbed down out of the truck he saw fire flying out of the windows of the two southerly buildings. Hurry. *Hurry.* Eldert trotted off to wound two more buildings: number four and number five. One to go, one to go; he chanted the slogan in his mind as he ran back to the truck; one to go, one to go; and it seemed to Eldert that he was growing stronger as he ran. He took up the only remaining incendiary device with both hands—the last one—and he was running away from the truck on the final delivery run when he saw the lights.

Oh, *no.* Aroni spotted a street number as he raced down Michigan Avenue and realized he'd gone a block or two too far. He managed a squealing left turn.

As Hammond rolled along the deserted side street, blinking lights danced rhythmically along buildings that lined the street. His old truck was the center of a small solar system moving through empty space. As he neared Indiana Avenue, Hammond worked the switch for the blinking lights and lost his escort. Now nothing else moved. But as soon as Hammond turned the corner—turned south on Indiana—several things were moving: a man running away from a truck that said *BUSY,* orange glow from buildings beyond, now the man dashing back toward the *BUSY* truck, lights coming up Indiana in the distance, *BUSY* truck beginning to *move.*

Numb.

He was caught like a deer in the approaching headlights, but only for those seconds when his heart could not beat. The heart did begin to pump again. Eldert dropped the silver-colored ball and bolted for the *BUSY* truck. He leaped inside the idling vehicle, worked the gearshift violently. The *BUSY* truck started forward. But the red truck coming at it from the north rolled up and banged into the front of the *BUSY* truck with teeth-rattling force. Eldert got the *BUSY* truck into reverse gear, stepped down frantically on the accelerator, and felt his *BUSY* truck lurch backward. Eldert yanked his head around to see where he was backing and saw lights coming up a block behind him. Panic took Eldert. He shifted into drive and tramped on the gas pedal and wrenched the wheel to steer around the red truck in front of him. But the driver of the red truck did the only thing he could think of to stop Eldert: Hammond stomped on his accelerator and steered straight into the *BUSY* truck. The force carried both vehicles up onto a sidewalk and threw them against a building. First the nightmare screams of metal rupturing. Then quieter sounds—bits of glass rattling down, liquids splashing—which were not clear over the sounds of the wind.

Eldert swallowed hard against a feeling he might vomit. He was dazed, but he could tell roughly where he was—somewhere on the opposite side of the street from buildings he had set afire—and he knew he had to try to move—*now*. He got his door open, got out onto the street. And he saw that somebody was getting out of the *other* truck. Eldert wheeled and moved off in a lurching run down Indiana. For only a few steps. He stopped and stared, puffing through his mouth. In the middle of the street ahead of him: headlamps, blinking amber lights, door open on the driver's side, someone getting *out*. He was *surrounded*, he believed, about to be taken. In his panicky state, Eldert did not guess that the man behind him was crippled and weaponless, the man in front old and weaponless. Eldert looked behind him to see if the man who had slammed into him was coming after him and saw that another vehicle had appeared: an auto with spinning Mars lights stood in the street near the tangle of trucks. Eldert saw movement there—at least two men. Dazed and terrified, Eldert fled to the one place he knew would receive him: the five-story warehouse full of paper boxes. He ran through the doorway—past the door he had pried open minutes before—and disappeared from sight.

Despite his bulk and despite the sling on his left arm, Dominic Benedetto led the charge after Eldert. Rosewater and Hooker were close behind. Hammond, on crutches, swung slowly along after them. Benedetto paused outside the doorway, drew his revolver, and eased the broken door open. He stepped back, pulling the door shut against the slap of hot air and smoke. He press-fit the revolver into its holster on his belt and looked quickly up and down the street. At the fires boiling furiously out of the buildings on this side of the street, at the old man holding a big press-type camera, at Hammond drawing near, at the two trucks locked in a frozen moment of combat, at the other two vehicles. Benedetto began barking orders. To Rosewater: "Take that car with the yella lights, get around behind, *stay* there. He may try to get out a window or door we can't see here. Make sure you get 'im if he does." To Aroni: "Give 'im your keys." To Hooker: "Get on the radio, call in half a dozen fires." Benedetto caught Hooker's shoulder with his right hand and looked at Hammond. "Anything else we need, Chief?"

Hammond said, "Rescue unit—with fire suits, if possible."

Benedetto looked to Hooker to see if Hooker heard, then released Hooker's shoulder and nodded. Hooker turned and trotted off toward the squad car. Benedetto looked to Hammond and asked, "Did he have a gun?"

Hammond shook his head and shouted, to be heard over the wind, "I don't know. I didn't see any."

Benedetto looked to Aroni, and Aroni shrugged and held a palm up. Benedetto looked into Aroni's eyes and told him, "You can stay, but keep back outta the way."

Even more in awe of Benedetto than of the things taking place around them, Aroni nodded dumbly and backpedaled.

Benedetto took hold of Hammond's upper arm and leaned close to talk with the drillmaster. "Chief, we need this sonofabitch—*alive*." Benedetto waited for Hammond's grim-faced nod to acknowledge the "alive" and then asked, "Can I get in there and get 'im?"

Hammond shook his head decisively. "That's a big building, and it's dark, full of smoke. Even if you had the gear to protect you, it's tough to find a guy who's hiding. Way the fire's spreading, I doubt the guy can last in there till some help gets here. I'd recommend you and Hooker keep your revolvers handy"—this partly to Hooker, who had rejoined them. "He may come flying out of there any second. If you have to—"

A window blew out overhead and showered glass out over the street, and flames shot out through the opening. Fourth floor. Hammond motioned the two policemen away, and they moved to the far side of the street. Glowing cinders came bounding along the street, hitting the pavement and leaping up, hitting the pavement and leaping, like a pack of foraging predators. Hammond shouted to Hooker to see if there was any protective headgear in either of the trucks. Another window blew out, and fire flew out in a sheet thirty feet long. Fourth floor. Now Hammond could see a fluctuating glow behind the large double-hung windows on the *fifth* floor. Fire was billowing out from buildings on both sides of this five-story warehouse; and even over the noise of the wind and the roar of the fire, they could hear a loud flapping sound—like flags or sails snapping in a heavy wind, a sound that fire sometimes makes when it is traveling fast. Hooker returned with just one safety hat, and Hammond motioned for him to put it on. He started to comply. The front door flew open, and Hooker moved like a track man coming off the blocks. He went to one knee and had his pistol up in two bandaged hands and pointed at the doorway. No one came out. The door had been thrown open by the fire, and it was obvious from the force of the flames inside the doorway that no one was coming through there. Hooker rose, replaced his revolver, and retrieved the hard hat, which he had tossed aside without a conscious thought. Another window blew out on the fourth floor. Hammond tapped Benedetto to get his attention, then pointed up. Both Benedetto and Hooker followed the line and saw it—saw *him:* Eldert Maddox stood at a fifth-floor window silhouetted by the flames behind him. Hammond reckoned that the man could not live more than a minute or two. If the man opened the window for air or broke it, the flames would roll over him like a waterfall, to get to the air. If he didn't, he would suffocate soon. Hammond thought about help on the way, but he could not hear sirens. Hammond yelled, "The net!" Neither policeman understood. Hammond shouted against the wind, *"The net. On the red truck. Get it."*

Benedetto understood and was already moving.

Hooker was uncertain about what he should be doing. He asked Hammond, "He need help?"

The drillmaster shook his head and looked back up to the fifth floor, where smoke was beginning to build up behind the windows. Was there some way, Hammond wondered, to ventilate the area up there or to draw the fire away from that man? He motioned for Hooker to bring his head close, and he asked in Hooker's ear, "Can you shoot out the last two windows on the end?" Hammond braced himself and pointed.

A backlighted Eldert Maddox could still be seen at a fifth-floor window. Heat waves rolling up from below made Eldert's silhouette seem to shimmy. Hooker saw that Hammond was pointing at fifth-floor windows farthest away from the trapped man. Hooker nodded. Hammond gave a silent order: He made his right hand into a pistol pointed at the windows and worked it.

Hammond paddled his crutches across the street to the accompaniment of pistol reports, the shattering of glass, and fire driving violently for the new air. Hammond could feel the heat increasing on his face as he crossed the street. He got to the spot where the net should go up no sooner than Benedetto did. Benedetto carried the rescue net, still folded but bulky and heavy, in his extended right hand. Not exactly the way we teach it at the Academy, thought Hammond. He motioned Hooker over to them and shouted instructions to the two men.

Eldert Maddox watched the net go up. So slowly. When you are burning to death, a minute goes on and on. Should he jump to those men down there? They would humiliate him, he thought; maybe kill him; they would look at his hands. Why not just—stay up here? Eldert's shirt caught fire. He screamed and leaped through the window—into space.

Piss on that big cop, Jules Aroni had decided. He had shot just one picture, had set his camera down on the street, and was coming up to help hold the net. He did not get there in time.

Dominic Benedetto had quite forgotten about the old photographer. He had been standing there wondering if he, Benedetto, with his terrible fear of heights, would be able to jump out a fifth-floor window at a doily in the street, when he realized his hair was burning. He started to remove his one usable hand from the frame of the net, but he kept his eyes on Hammond's face.

• 186 •

Vernon Hooker kept a tight grip on the frame. He was not thinking about his burned hands. He was concentrating on the two things the chief had told him to do: keep his knees flexed and keep his eyes on Hammond.

Seconds earlier, Robert Hammond had lifted his elbows and let the crutches fall away. He had his face turned up to watch for the jumper and also to watch for falling debris. Was this the man who murdered Sheri Sue, the man who wanted to kill Hammond too? Move this net to one side or the other and he'd end up looking like that watermelon thrown off the drill hall. Hammond tried to force the thoughts out of his mind. He saw the man's body come out the window, and he yelled at the two policemen to move a step to his right.

The flaming object fell for almost two seconds, and it hit the net with incredible force—nearest Benedetto—and flipped around. The force hammered the net and the three men holding it onto the ground, knocking the men unconscious, *breaking* them.

The photographer was smothering the fire that had had the man on the net twisting in pain when the first two pieces of fire-fighting equipment rolled up. Firemen called for ambulances, removed the net, and bent low over the four bodies to look for signs of life. Three of the four men were still alive.

A man reached for Dominic Benedetto's penis.

"What the hell're you *doin'* there?" demanded Benedetto.

"Is *this* tender?" asked the intern.

Benedetto sucked in air sharply and arched his hips up off the table.

"Thought so," mumbled the intern. Then he grinned reassuringly at Benedetto and said, "Don't worry, Big. You're still in business."

"Ohh," said the nurse. She had just cut one of the gloves away and had been jolted by the sight of what was inside. An intern who was standing a few feet away looked over his shoulder at the nurse and followed her gaze to Eldert's mutilated left hand. He laid down the instruments he was holding and stepped over to have a closer look. "Good God Al-might-y," he whispered. He slipped his hand under Eldert's left hand and lifted it, then turned it carefully from side to side, studying it. He laid the hand back on the table, lifted one of Eldert's eyelids, then the other, and made a swift check of Eldert's nearly nude body. "Poor bastard," he said. "If people could see what fire can do to human flesh—" He stopped in midsentence because the nurse was just cutting the glove away from Eldert's right hand. The intern shook his head and said, "This guy wasn't hurt much this time, but he sure as hell was ruined sometime in the past."

The curtain that formed the walls of an emergency-room cubicle parted enough for Dominic Benedetto to pass through. Benedetto was nearly bald, and slings now held *both* his arms. He walked the three feet to the bed in half a dozen steps—*miniature* steps—and said, "Chief?"

Hammond's eyes were not working as they should, and he was heavily drugged to mask the pain in his left leg, but he recognized the massive figure creeping toward him. Hammond grinned and said, "Good to hear—way you're walk—'fraid you be a soprano."

Benedetto sounded his rumbling laugh and said, "Next time, Chief, get somebody else help you hold up yer goddamn net. What's wrong with yer eyes?"

"Jus' little well done. How's Hooker?"

Benedetto set his lips for a moment. He started to speak: "Hooks—" He blinked hard. Then he quit blinking and let the tears come and roll down his dark face.

23

AFTERWORD

WHEN the sun rose the next morning, the people of Chicago couldn't see it because of a substratum of smoke that hung over the city, seemingly supported by a thousand thin stalagmites of smoke which rose from scattered dying fires. In some neighborhoods, nothing stood up over three feet from the blackened ground. Nothing. And when people returned to try to find the ruins of their properties, they would first have to try to find the *streets*. In early morning, the great city was curiously quiet, as if a church service were in progress.

The newspapers were so fat with photos it was as if the editors had finally given up trying to choose among them and decided to throw them all in. But one photo stood out from all the rest: an affecting picture of three damaged men—two bandaged policemen staring intently at a bandaged and trouserless fireman, who was looking up—just the three of them holding up a net as well as they could while the destruction whirled about them. This particular photo ran, as a wire-service photo, in a third of all the papers in the country. Seeing it, more than one cynical Chicagoan swallowed hard.

Many Chicagoans sat before their TV sets endlessly, as absorbed in the tenth telling as in the first. Content to hear the same story over and over; like a child, *preferring* to. Death toll, injuries, property damage, jobs lost, activities canceled, special church services, disaster relief available to victims, pleas to stay away from ravaged areas, threats to would-be looters. Least appreciated were interviews of politicians. What some viewers found most absorbing were the graphic explanations of how the Red Wind had formed; how it had moved; why it had shifted in direction, then died away with about one third of the city destroyed; and why probably nothing could have stood up to it, given the physical conditions.

But many Chicagoans were looking for *meta*physical explanations. To have seen the Red Wind—actually to have *seen* it—was to have been dumbfounded. Even those who saw only the ravages afterward were awestruck. Had the Red Wind been directed by a conscious Satanic personality? Had the Ruler of Heaven and Earth made an individual decision to spare the life of each individual survivor for a special purpose? Some, despite losing most or all of their possessions, felt lucky and rich. Some wanted to join with others to give thanks. Some mourned for victims. Some had time on their hands because their jobs had blown away on the wind, and they were apprehensive about the future. Some were eager simply to be where people congregated. For all of these reasons, churches had standing-room-only attendance.

Hammond awakened to the sound of bells. His eyes were seared and swollen shut. The only one with him was an armed guard.

Minot Winston Gault III absently noticed the man's suit; he *recognized* it; it was the same suit the man had worn—what was it?—four, five days ago when he had come here to see Gault. It was a quite unremarkable dark blue suit, but Gault noticed such things without consciously trying to.

The visitor made his report in a quiet voice: "Nobody caused that collapse, Commissioner. That stuff came down on Chief Hammond by accident. I'm sure of it." The policeman paused, then added in a flat voice, "It would appear that Lieutenant Benedetto's action was rather heroic, actually."

Gault said, "I'm very relieved to hear it. And I'll tell Commissioner Keller we're indebted for your help. Now, Captain, may I ask you a *personal* question? Off the record?"

"Yes, sir." Again that flat tone.

"You're not a big fan of Lieutenant Benedetto, are you?"

"No, sir."

Gault pressed the matter carefully: "But you're pretty certain now that Benedetto didn't do this thing to Chief Hammond."

"I know he didn't," said the visitor matter-of-factly. "We did check everything out thoroughly, Commissioner, but I knew from the start what we'd find."

Gault leaned forward. "Can you tell me how?"

The big visitor averted his eyes for a moment, thinking. Then he looked at Gault's eyes and asked, "In absolute confidence, Commissioner?"

"That's agreed, Captain."

The visitor touched his fingertips lightly to the ruined landscape that was the left side of his face. He tried a casual smile but let it go. He spoke slowly and did not look at Gault. "A guy who can break your face when you've got three other men helping you—a guy like that doesn't do a sneaky act like this. Two of the guys who were helping me, they were hospitalized, and one of 'em eventually took early retirement because he didn't heal right." The visitor made a humorless smile. "Hell, he looks even worse than *I* do. Some guys have shunned Benedetto 'cause they think he attacked *us*." The visitor made a throwaway gesture with his hand, as if to tell Gault that what was coming next really didn't matter. "We were sore 'cause Benedetto complained about— about the way we treated some suspects, we thought we'd teach him a lesson. Well, that big bastard is not easy to teach." Now the visitor looked directly at Gault and said, "The big problem with Benedetto, he never could bend a rule if it was life and death."

Dominic Benedetto was certain he knew who had made the anonymous call to his wife Saturday morning. Whoever it was (a) had sounded like a man, (b) had somehow found out (or suspected) that the fat man was behind the fires, (c) knew that Benedetto was involved in the investigation, and (d) wanted to give Ruck's name to him instead of to Hammond but (e) didn't want to come forward and tell *how* he (she?) knew. Why a call to his *home?* Maybe the informant was afraid of recording devices on police phones. Maybe a lot of things. These circumstances might have suggested an underworld figure or maybe a trust officer who had seen through Ruck's elaborate efforts at secrecy, had not the detective's mind already been sniffing at another door. Four bugles paid well enough, but Gold Coast? After Hammond had asked to be left alone in his bathroom Saturday afternoon, Benedetto had detailed a man to keep an eye on him and had made quick calls to D. Dexter Denning (about Hammond's condominium) and to an art dealer (about the Braque). Numbers that would blow your hat off. Income from writing and teaching evening classes? Hardly. Inheritance? Later calls revealed that Hammond had bought the flat shortly after his marriage had broken up and about the time Sid Ruck cleared out of Chicago. At first, there was only the suspicion. Benedetto decided to include Hammond in the investigation, at least nominally, so he could keep an eye on him. If Hammond was as tired and tortured as he looked, Benedetto guessed he might not have long to wait. Even so, he was a little surprised at how soon it had come and more surprised that he felt a sense of loss when it did come. That very same evening, Hammond had quietly, unwittingly given himself away. Dennis Rosewater had asked what kind of company Ruck owned, and Benedetto had told him it was one of those board-up outfits. Benedetto could still hear it just the way the drillmaster had said it: "You've probably seen their trucks around fires. They say *BUSY*." Well, Benedetto hadn't told him that, and with more than forty board-up companies in Chicago, it was no guess.

Proving it would be tough, maybe impossible; Sid Ruck was dead, and the fire had taken Hammond's condo, his personal papers, his Braque. But to Benedetto, the point was that he *knew,* and the question was what he was going to do about it. Put Hammond in prison if he could or, failing that, break him and run him out of Chicago? Benedetto remembered the pain in Hammond's eyes on Saturday, remembered the poor sonofabitch bawling and raving in the hospital last night; no doubt Hammond could be hurt some more, but Benedetto wondered how much more. A young arson investigator had taken money several years ago at a time when his personal life was in turmoil. Would Benedetto's attitude about a proper punishment be different if Hammond's act of corruption back then weren't linked to multiple deaths and massive destruction now? Did that corrupt act define the man's whole life? Hammond had tipped Ruck early Saturday morning—that was before he knew anything about Sheri Sue's death or anything about an attempt on his own life or anything about the big fire coming; he had telephoned Benedetto's wife even though he had to know he was putting his own neck in jeopardy. And Hammond had risked his own safety again to save a hideous creep he had to want dead. The drillmaster knew a couple of things about duty.

Even if justice, whatever the hell that is, needed Hammond's ass, Benedetto speculated, what about what *Chicago* needed? Another scandal involving a public official? Chief Hammond was, if not a hero, at least a hero *figure*—something Chicago had desperate need of. And an authority on arson. He's going to make me a hell of an assistant, the policeman decided.

The first bells had begun to sound just before 9:00 A.M. Soon other bells joined them. By noon every bell in Chicago and most of those in the suburbs were chiming and gonging and clanging. They rang until after dark. After that, the city seemed a little too quiet. But not for long.

Tomorrow the bulldozers would move in. Debris would be used to extend the lakeshore. Just as it was in 1871.

There will probably never be another fire like the one which destroyed Chicago in 1871. However, unless something is done to improve arson prevention and investigation, the result could be almost the same—a city under fire.

—*The Chicago Reporter,* Vol. 7, No. 2, February 1978

People thought that as it had got among the brick and stone it would be retarded. . . . Engines seemed entirely useless. The long tongues of flame would dart out over a whole block, then come back and lap it all up clean. Iron and stone seemed to come down as in a blast furnace.

—Excerpt from October 14, 1871, letter written by a Chicago high school principal, George Howland, as quoted in The Chicago Historical Society's *The Great Chicago Fire,* Chicago, 1971.

. . . Joseph Medill, by campaigning on the issue of fire prevention, was elected mayor in 1872. But I live in a large frame house that was built in the burned district in 1875, and many of my neighbors occupy frame structures erected later. In fact, the area is so vulnerable to fire that the Chicago Fire Department dispatches five pieces of apparatus in response to every alarm, and throws them in fast. Thus slowly do we human beings turn experience to advantage!

—Excerpt from Paul M. Angle's introduction to Robert Cromie's *The Great Chicago Fire.* New York: McGraw-Hill Book Company, 1958.